When the Beckett family of Johannesburg, South Africa, packed beach towels for the summer holiday they did not intend spending the ensuing weeks acquainting themselves with broiling desert roadsides, embattled third-world hospitals, or the intimate civic pathology of some of the least tourist-attractive towns on earth. Ah hah. They had reckoned without their car. Umpteen breakdowns later, journalist Denis Beckett had discovered an eighth wonder of the world: The Unreliable Vehicle, without which homo bourgeoians would proceed eternally from A to B according to schedule. In the pages of *The Road Stops At Nowhere*, adventure story meets applied philosophy and travel tale intersects with socio-political enquiry. Three weeks overlap into timelessness; South Africa's special peculiarities bump into the universal human predicament.

The Road Stops At Nowhere

Denis Beckett

PENGUIN BOOKS

PENGUIN BOOKS

Published by the Penguin Group
27 Wrights Lane, London W8 5TZ, England
Viking Penguin, a division of Penguin Books USA Inc, 375 Hudson Street,
New York, New York 10014, USA
Penguin Books Australia Ltd, Ringwood, Victoria, Australia
Penguin Books Canada Ltd, 10 Alcorn Avenue, Toronto, Ontario,
Canada M4V 3B2
Penguin Books (NZ) Ltd, Cnr Rosedale and Airborne Roads, Albany,
Auckland, New Zealand
Penguin Books (South Africa) (Pty) Ltd, 1A Eton Road, Parktown
South Africa 2193

Penguin Books (South Africa) (Pty) Ltd, Registered Offices:
1A Eton Road, Parktown, South Africa 2193

First published by NDA Press, a Division of News Design Associates, Inc,
This edition first published by Penguin, 1998

ISBN 0 140 28242 4

Designed and typeset in Kennerley Oldstyle and News Gothic by News Design Associates, Inc
Illustrations: Rui Ramalheiro
Map: Edwin Taylor
Map inset: Bernard Bennell
Printed and bound by The Rustica Press, Old Mill Road, Ndabeni
D6742

For Meave, Emma, and Matt, in hope
that they and their wavering peers will never be blinded
to the sometimes veiled rewards wrapped
in the challenges of Africa; and for Kyle Anthony,
for whom may the world ever remain innocent

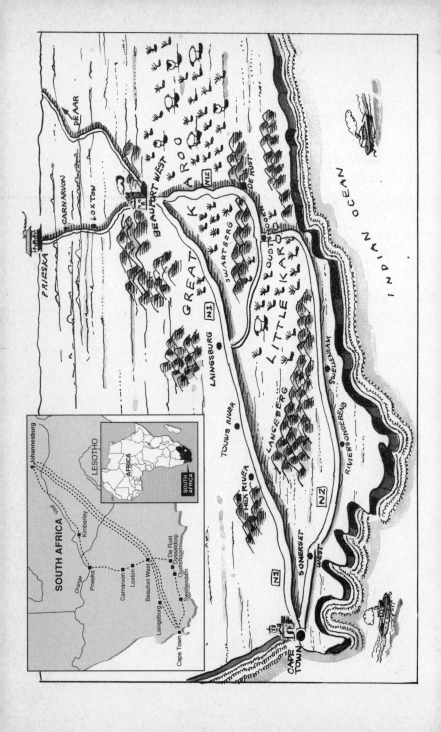

Prescript

IF YOU SCRUTINISE A MAP OF SOUTH AFRICA, NOT THAT I imagine this is a daily pursuit, you will find a large dot-free chunk around the south western part. This is a semi-desert called the Karoo, one of the gentler eczemas upon the epidermis of the Earth.

The Karoo is a timid desert, as deserts go. It lacks the gripping parched image of Man against the Elements, the lonely doomed figure clawing across dunes while hyenas lick their lips. It's a 70% desert, which is nowhere. Its next-door neighbours the Kalahari and the Namib relegate it to second league even before you get to the Skeleton Coast, which does the job by name alone.

So, for most people the mental compartment the Karoo occupies is in the cobwebbed section. Me, too. It was the long dull stretch on the way to the Cape beaches. Then in the closing hours of 1989 the insides of my automobile were apparently bewitched, and I spent the opening weeks of the 1990s getting to know the Karoo rather more closely than scheduled.

This was a particularly strange time, even in a country where all times are strange. This was the opening of the interregnum. After 347 years of various forms of white rule, white rule was on the point of the deep dive. The old order was passing, and nobody had any idea of where to now. Hardly anybody even knew what the central figure of the new age, a 27-year-long prisoner named Nelson Mandela, looked like.

Public and media discussion, within South Africa as well as about South Africa, was all to do with change and politics and so forth. In the Karoo, I felt, I was seeing something different — a slice of a nation's soul, reaching beneath and beyond the topical flurry.

Back at home I felt the urge to pound the keyboard and tell it as it had been. Trouble was, what to do with the 13,000 words that resulted. At the time, I was running a magazine called *Frontline*, which was terrifically high-minded and anti-apartheid and so forth, and occasionally banned, but *Frontline* was, y'know, serious. It was about saving the nation, not about recalcitrant engines. Also, being noble, it was of course broke and therefore what is euphemistically known as "slim." 13,000 words would crowd out everything else. None of the better-off journals seemed filled with anxiety to make space for an unclassifiable amalgam of dusty travelogue and soft sociology, so the tale of car and Karoo was pointed for a lonely career in a bottom drawer.

But the Law of Perverse Outcomes was not to be flouted. Shortly afterwards, *Frontline's* lousy finances having descended to a new low, I relinquished the editorial role (which I loved) in order to focus on money matters (which I hated). My stand-in was a remarkable American, Don Caldwell, who had adopted South Africa and by the time of his death in a car crash two years later was an extremely distinctive fish in the local pond. Don's strongest suit was zest, and when he stumbled upon the Karoo story the zest came on fierce. "We must publish it," he said.

"We can't," I replied, "it's like the proprietor of *The New York Times* filling an edition with his family holiday."

"Rubbish," said Don, "this'll be our best edition, now go away and find something to pay the printer with."

Don persuaded persuasively. We ran the Karoo story and a funny thing happened. Over the next month or so we had 260 letters in reply. Nobody in media work is flooded by letters, like everybody else thinks they are. Cocktail comments, maybe, and street-corner nudges, but trouble-taking pen-to-paper responses are few and far between, and usually angry. Here we had fifty times more response than to a normal edition, and hardly any of it was angry. The Karoo had struck some sort of chord.

By January of 1998 the echoes had faded to nothingness and I reckoned the Karoo saga was well and truly history.

Then Tony Sutton had a brainwave. Tony, having started life as an Englishman, spent 15 years in South Africa where he became a guru of newspaper and magazine production and designed, among other things, all but a handful of the 106 editions *Frontline* notched up. (One of that handful, by Murphy's Law, was the Karoo edition). Then he picked on Canada and set up a consultancy, News Design Associates, operating on the slogan that his company's work "makes good things better."

Now he wanted the Karoo story to be one of the good things he would make better. I was honoured, but a little perplexed. The Karoo was an awfully long way from the snow and civilisation of Toronto. Could Tony see his super-literate readers getting wrapped up in the lives and hard times of a bunch of desert-dwellers at the bottom end of a forgotten continent?

"Yes," he said, "the story isn't just about the Karoo, it's about the world."

Maybe there's something in that. Maybe there's a way in which our funny little third-world squabbles hold within them a certain inspiration, along with the farce and the tragedy and the disbelieving hand clapped to the long-suffering brow. We down here in our improbable concatenation of four races and umpteen ethnic groups are frequently considered one of the world's sad cases, not least by ourselves, and particularly by our professional classes whose height of ambition is Sydney, Australia.

Extreme heterogeneity does indeed present stresses, with incidents and events that make you want to throw up. At the same time, though, it also presents a heck of a lot of challenge, and some special rewards.

For me, there is a dimension to life here that would not be the same in the places where the streets are neat and crime is discreet and people share language and accent and collective memory and conventions about which side of the soup plate to tip up.

The down sides in Africa are steep as the cliffs of Hades. But the up sides — the getting to know, the coming to terms, the ways of sharing, with people entirely unlike yourself — can be a wonder of the world.

Maybe that relates to why Tony picked on the Karoo story.

Tony is becoming the Gulley Jimson of modern publishing. Gulley, the hero of Joyce Carey's *The Horse's Mouth,* was an artist for whom the meaning and purpose of life was to paint, and the thing to be painted was a wall. Gulley appreciated a fine wall like some men appreciate a fine woman or a fine horse. When he met a good wall he had to paint it, in complete disregard of petty practical considerations such as who owned it.

Tony is like that when it comes to publishing. When he sees the right writing he has to publish it, in complete disregard of petty practical considerations such as outlay and income. Thus is the planet enriched. It needs its Gulleys, and its Tonys.

Denis Beckett,
Johannesburg, June 1998

Preface to the Penguin edition

A SOUTH AFRICAN VERSION OF A CANADIAN BOOK BASED ON A South African magazine article … is that otherwise or what? Well, it's what you've got. This edition of this book is approx 98% on sale below the Limpopo. The beginning and the end, and the numerous footnotes, were written for readers to whom the Limpopo, and everything southwards, is some distant planet. We thought of dropping those bits but then re-thought: No, there's something alluring for our own people too, in seeing what is being explained to the buitelanders.

Khotso! Sterkte!

Denis Beckett,
Johannesburg, September 1998

Friday

GRAAAAAAK.

Just like that. Out of the blue. One minute we're happily humming through the heat-haze of Karoo air rising from the tarmac. Next minute there's an awful racket and the engine dies a death. We're halfway up a long hill. I roll the car back to a thorn-tree which offers the only shade available. The family compresses into its limited shelter while I scour the engine with a stern eye. The only eggs in the car are hard-boiled. A pity, as we would like to ascertain whether a Karoo roadside in midsummer can serve as a frying pan. We have our suspicions.

A Samaritan materialises, in the form of an army chaplain from Namibia. We lash our broken Mitsubishi Starwagon behind his Landrover and cover the 40 miles to Beaufort West in half an hour, praying that he has no cause for a sudden stop.

Then come the peaks and troughs of mechanical diagnosis.

"Ag, it's nothing," says the mechanic, "a broken timing belt. You'll be on the road in an hour."

Relief — until it's discovered that the oil pump has also broken. Is there one around?

Ah, here we are. Elation.

Oops, it doesn't fit. Gloom.

Maybe Koos[1] can dig one up. Hope.

Koos succeeds; it fits. Elation.

Uh oh, the pistons are also seized. Gloom. Parts must come from Cape Town, about to close for the Cape's peculiar four-day New Year weekend.

We're on a family holiday and have rented an isolated cottage in the Eastern Cape, way off public transport routes. Word spreads that we're in need of wheels. A dealer produces a weary Peugeot, the only hire car in town. "Take it," he urges. "Take it right now, because someone is clamouring for it. He's waiting at my office, money in his hand."

"So why not give it to him? He was first."

"He's black."

When we decline, offers of sale and trade-in pitch up. Motor dealers converge and ferry me back and forth to inspect used cars. Everybody tells me why everybody else's offer is no good, and most also take time to point out the town's attractions: Chris Barnard's father's church, Chris Barnard's birthplace, and the Chris Barnard[2] museum.

"And that's not all," says a proud townsman, miffed that the tourist trade underrates Beaufort West, "we also have a lot of sheep farming we can show people."

By close of business several motor traders are gathered in a tiny garage office waiting for us to make our choice. Finally we reject all offers. We've phoned my parents near Cape Town; they've urged us to divert to them. We tell the traders we'll make for Cape Town, by train. There's a moment of disappointment. "Ag," sighs one man, "if only we Beauforters could learn to pull together — at least one of us could have made a sale." But our decision

---

1. Abbreviation of Jakobus, pronounced halfway between "Kwos" and "Quoors."
2. Chris, the world's first heart-transplanter, is still household material in South Africa, although I suppose a dimming name elsewhere.

disposes of the commercial tensions. A bottle emerges from a filing cabinet, and there's an impromptu party. Someone rings the railways to book us seats, but that can't be done. The train is already under way, so we must wait till it arrives and ask the conductor. "Jeez," says the garage man, "don't these railways ous[3] know about computers?"

We have a chaotic combi[4]-load of bags and blankets and buckets and spades to get to the station. A dealer hands us the keys to a show car. He's never seen us before, he doesn't know our name, he gives us the keys and says to leave them with the stationmaster.

When the Trans-Karoo trundles in at 9.20, the station is packed. Third-class passengers climb aboard freely. Second-class passengers mob the conductor, who ignores the crush and unhurriedly mounts a podium like a preacher on a pulpit. He calls out the pre-booked:

"Engelbrecht!"

"Hier."

"12G. Visagie!"

"Hier."

"9F."

Then it is the turn of the unbooked, gathered at his feet. Everybody is beaming ingratiatingly at the conductor and vying to catch his eye. It is tacitly accepted that our three small children give our claim top status, but that will be no use if there are no spare berths. The station master has predicted there are probably not, and I gird my loins to fight for the right to travel third class, which I do not expect the conductor to lightly let a white family do. The station master was wrong. All the white applicants are allocated bunks with no difficulty. Then there is one person left, the only

---

3. "Chap" or "fellow," from "ou kerel," "old boy."
4. What the manufacturers, mainly VW, call "microbus," but South Africans stick to the old abbreviation from "combination" (car and van) with the same tenacity as we stick to "robot" for "traffic light."

coloured.

"Nothing," says the conductor, "but you can travel third." The coloured guy is about 30, slender and bespectacled and exuding the whiff of refinement. "I'd rather travel second," he says.

"Coloured second-class is full," shrugs the conductor, and turns away.

Loaded up, I go to the ticket office to make us legal. The coloured guy is standing on the platform, expressionless and alone. I presume he feels that third class would not be safe for him. Funny, I could put my white face and family in there more confidently than he could. We'd be amusing oddities; he stands to be accused of putting on airs. He faces a 24-hour wait, I suppose, but I'm not about to be taking up cudgels for railway desegregation on Beaufort West Platform 1. "Best of luck," I say, lamely. He looks through me.

The ticket office tells me I buy my tickets on the train. Well, if that's the way it is, who am I to argue? I climb aboard and we wave farewell to Beaufort. In due course the conductor comes round and an odd exchange follows. The conductor speaks in hints and riddles, working out slow sums on the back of a cigarette box. I'm expecting a simple flat price. I feel I am somehow being frustratingly naive, but I don't know why. Afterwards I realise I have handed over R231[5] in cash and have nothing to show for it — no ticket, no receipt. A query seeps slowly into mind: Does SA Transport Services get to see my money? Ah, ridiculous! Must have been a mistake. The railways are straight. Everybody knows that. The railways! This is Calvinism on wheels. Conductors don't do back-pocket deals. Do they?

---

5. *Perhaps $90 at the time, and about a day-and-a-half's income for a genteelly penurious social-conscience publisher.*

Two Weekends And Inbetween

ONCE I CRASHED A TRUCK IN DUBLIN, NEXT TO A GARAGE. "Can you fix it?" I asked the jovial proprietor.

"Ah sure and I can fix it by tomorra with no trouble at all."

Amazing, I thought. Who said these Irish were tardy? I asked for his phone number and he said he'd forgotten. Forgotten? Yes, he said, it's been out of order so long.

I leave it to late tomorra before I catch the two buses across town to pick up the truck. It hasn't been touched.

"What was the problem?"

"Ah sure," and he looks so crestfallen you want to give him a heartening pat, "and I couldn't get the parts."

"Well, er, when exactly can you get the parts?"

"Ah sure and finished tomorra with no trouble at all, at all."

I catch my two buses home and tomorra I catch them back and the truck is gathering dust and the story is identical. On the third day it's the same and I blow up. "You knew it wouldn't be ready today, so why did you say it would?" He was sorely aggrieved. "Ah sure," he said, "and didn't I want you to have a happy evening?"

That was Ireland in the late '70s. In Beaufort West in the early '90s they work on a similar principle. They have a phone but don't believe in outgoing calls, so I phone daily from Cape Town for progress reports. The mechanic is invariably under an engine and disrupts operations with much audible cursing.

The car is due to be ready by Thursday, and then it's Friday and then it's Monday and day by day the list of replacement parts expands until it fills three pages of my notebook with mind-numbing implications for my bankbook. Finally Tuesday is the day.

"For sure?"

"Yes, meneer, absolutely definitely for sure, definite."

Fine, then, so Tuesday it'll be the family on the Trans-Karoo to Beaufort West, collect the car and off to the rented cottage in the Eastern Province.

All cut and dried. Except that on Monday afternoon our eight-year-old breaks her arm.

Monday

WHEN A FREAK FALL LEAVES A LITTLE GIRL WITH A LIMB looking like two sides of a triangle, what you do is, you rush to the nearest hospital. This was Victoria, in the Cape Town suburb of Wynberg.

I have known general hospitals, from times like the rainy night long ago when a truck came between me and my motorbike. The ambulancemen were still wheeling me in when people in white coats fell upon me and got the repair job under way.

That is the image I have in mind as we hurtle from the Atlantic coast up and over Constantia Nek, one of the most beautiful passes in the Cape Peninsula or anywhere else.

Some chance. Casualty at Victoria is packed. In the scale of urgency, a broken arm ranks near an ingrowing toenail. There is heavy stuff here. People are wheeled past us, unconscious and mangled and bloody, life expectancies looking measurable in minutes.

Last I knew, Victoria was a white hospital. It certainly can't be called a white hospital now, but it can't reasonably be called a nonracial hospital either. The law might say it's nonracial but in practice it's a racial hospital all over again, now a coloured one. The only white patients in sight are a couple of characters you'd expect to find in the magistrates court, with No Fixed Abode on the charge sheet.

The throng is 90% decent people waiting with the patience of the rock of ages, and 10% loud drunken low-grade gomtorrels[6] who swill liquor and use the floor as a dustbin and play clashing music at crazy volumes on their tapedecks. Ambulances are in and out like racing cars at pitstops. A police van brings in a handcuffed man who you hope you'll never meet in a dark street.

A ramshackle Datsun skids dangerously into the emergency bay and disgorges a furious woman and a bloodied baby. Four drunk men sprawl in the car, which stays in the ambulance bay. They're knocking back beer in quart bottles, spitting slimy gobs out of their open doors. One tosses a bottle over his shoulder. It narrowly misses a wheelchair patient and shatters on the tarmac.

Nobody can make out what we're doing there. It's not hard to see why. We might think that we're plain folks, but in this context that's a ludicrous affectation. Here we're larneys[7] like it or not, and the only other people who look and talk like us are wearing stethoscopes or thermometers. The staff and their patients look at us quizzically, like at a pin-stripe in a soup kitchen queue.

Sisters, bustling by, assure us that nothing bad is happening inside that broken arm, and then bustle on to the newest emergency.

Top needs get top priority. At the other extreme, several patients— evidently need company more than treatment and are constantly shoved to

---

6. *"Low calibre persons" if you like, or any of many synonyms. In Afrikaans, with its guttural "g," "o" like a punch in the stomach, and rough two-stroke "r," you can pack a lot of disdain into a word like gomtorrel.*

7. *Originally lahnee, used by Indians to mean white people. Now generally used by unfancy people to apply to fancy people — the kind who seem to have gone to private school and/or university.*

the back of the queue. That is clearly where most of them want to be, in the whirl of the waiting room for as long as possible before they are dispatched back to their loneliness. For the rest of us — with definite but not mortal medical needs — first-come, first-served is adhered to about as rigidly as is possible in the crush.

We're sent to X-ray. The sister says to take a stretcher and wheel it ourselves, as there's nobody else to wheel it. That's fine by us. We'd pass up the stretcher altogether, but no, it's Regulations. We lose our way a few times. The X-rays are done fast and with wondrous bedside manner, and then it's back to Casualty and finally the big moment: The Doctor.

The doctor is young and pleasant and perfectly knowledgeable, the kind of graduate the University of Cape Town should be proud of. But he's oddly disconnected, as if his mind keeps slipping gear or wafting away and he has to repeatedly wrench it back into place. Something's wrong; we can't work out what.

The break needs an orthopaedic surgeon, says the doctor. He and the sisters battle to find one, sending beeper calls around the peninsula in stolen seconds between stitching and treating the flood of ailing bodies. But as beep after beep fails to produce results we develop Plan B from the callbox, invoking grandparently contacts with a private clinic an hour away on the other side of False Bay. The doctor writes us a referral.

That he writes it surprises us. Half of Wynberg is clamouring for him, people with broken heads and bits of bottle stuck in their insides, and he's busy with a superfluous report to an unknown specialist who will toss it away and look at the X-rays.

What surprises us more is how he writes it. He can't write it. The pen is all over the page; he can't get time or date right; everything is misspelled — weird misspellings like repetition of syllyllables. We realise what's wrong. He is all but sleep-walking. He has been at work so long he doesn't know which side is up. In the course of thankyous we say it seems a fellow could take some strain around here. Tears well in his eyes and trickle down his cheeks as he staggers off.

We depart Victoria in less rush than we arrived, and chilled with respect. These people deserve medals. Medals and sleep and gigantic incomes.

The private clinic is smooth and humming, so far removed from the turmoil and urine-stench of an hour ago that it's hard to believe the two institutions are in the same line of business.

One reason for the calm is the sign at the portal: NO CASUALTY. The other is medical aid.

Everybody with medical aid keeps right out of the public hospitals, and that means nearly all whites, a hang of a lot of coloureds, and an expanding advance guard of blacks. So what you get in the private hospitals is a bizarre class inversion: All the blacks are high-class, the coloureds stretch down to middle, and the whites include anyone but the No Fixed Abodes.

Admission is by interrogation. One question is whether we mind sharing a ward with a coloured lady, who turns out to be the very model of everybody's favourite aunt. Then a million medical questions. The orthopod decrees a general anaesthetic, and nurse after nurse comes to check on diabetes, allergies, etc. A nurse apologises for fussing. By us, she can ask questions all night. A friend died a year ago when an anaesthetist took things too casually. The fussier everybody is, the better.

One question is asked all night. Ascending ranks of official call in to say: "Excuse me, there seems to be an error. This form indicates that you have no medical aid."

I say: "That's right, no medical aid," and they blink and breathe deep. If we hadn't slipped in the back way, contacting the surgeon through mutual friends, we might still be hammering at the front door.

During the pre-med, a white lady in the next ward starts raising cain. She strides belligerent and semi-dressed along the corridor, paining the ears of her mainly prim and mainly coloured fellow patients with loud foul language. I don't suppose anybody gets asked if they mind sharing with her.

Before the small hours are out, the arm is set and plastered. But to be at the station by daybreak is not a great option in the circumstances.

So Tuesday's Trans-Karoo is short of five passengers, and that's just as well. When I phone Beaufort West to let the garage know, I hear that a new problem has arisen. A water-pump. Another R324. The car is to be ready by Wednesday night, for sure, definite.

Strategy is updated. I will fetch the car alone, bring it to Cape Town to collect the family, and then we'll drive to the Eastern Province to put in a token two days at the cottage we'd rented for two weeks.

Wednesday

I'M SHARING A TRANS-KAROO COMPARTMENT WITH A PRISON warder, a soldier, a German tourist and a matric boy from De Aar.

The warder outlines the hardships of a warder's life, mainly a serious lack of appreciation on the part of the wardees. He then spruces up and leaves to choon[8] chicks. We see him no more.

The soldier joined the army a year ago and is bored to death, so is quitting to join the air force. He falls asleep in a top bunk and snores all the way.

The German is a technician on holiday, with a bioscope[9] accent. He wanted sunshine and got to South Africa because the travel agent said here was where his money would stretch furthest.[10]

----

8. *To tune chicks (rendered in local phonetics) is SA shorthand for "seek the acquaintance of damsels."*

9. *The term people used for cinemas in the days when movie Germans were always caricatures.*

10. *Dead right too. Our rand has shrunk even further since, more because of the world's lack of faith in Africa than because of actual failings of our economy, with the result that tourists can have 5-star holidays here for prices that would mean a back-room walk-up in the cosy countries.*

At Touws Rivier, he is looking out the window while I am engrossed in a brilliant account of the life and times of a stripper called Blaze Starr in the *Washington Post Magazine* and wondering why South African journalism can't touch this calibre.

He pulls his head back and says: "Excuss me. I do not vant to be political but ziss is vat is wrong viss your country." A hefty uniformed official, white, with clipboard in hand and half an inch of hair-oil on head, is striding past. A tiny coloured man is reeling behind under three enormous sacks.

"Excuss me," says the German, "I do not vant to be political but vy can't ze fat man carry even vun of ze bags?"

The schoolboy is a walking guidebook. His father is on the railways and he knows the line rail by rail. Karoo bred, he's high with pride and takes it as his duty to enlighten these foreigners — he evidently perceives Munich and Johannesburg as about equidistant from his world.

He has virtually no English, and none that survives the German's accent. I discover the power of the interpreter's role. At one barren dorp[11] the German wonders how anybody can live in a place like this. The boy looks at me, bright-eyed and keenly awaiting an interesting observation on his beloved Karoo. I adjust the remark to a compliment on the arid majesty of the landscape. The boy beams from ear to ear at a very puzzled German.

I'm puzzled myself by the boy's non-existent English, especially since he says his school is dual medium. But it emerges that what he means is boys and girls go to the same classes.

The train reaches Beaufort West at six in the evening. According to plan, the garage will be waiting for me, and I'll take the car and go.

I am not greatly surprised to find the workshop closed. The petrol attendants say the mechanic lives nearby, but when I ask for specifics all I get is nervous giggles. Mystified, I turn to passers-by of the white persuasion.

---

11. *Small town.*

Third time lucky: A man knows the mechanic and knows where he lives.

"But," he says, "be careful that side, hey. It's next to the spookhuis." A haunted house? I think he's joking. But no; he pinpoints the spookhuis, soberly, and says to be sure to be gone by dark.

I look out for a dank and dismal tower, but the spookhuis is stone ordinary except that the doors are closed.

The mechanic isn't bothered by the spookhuis, or about delivery dates either. There was a slip-up, but the water-pump will be along in the morning, ten o'clock on the goods train, and then only half an hour to finish the job.

"Fine. So I can be on the road at 10.30?"

"Ja, well, no, not really, it takes until quarter to one to get the package from the station."

"1.15, then?"

"Well, not exactly. That's lunch. Say 2.15. Perhaps 2.30. Or 3.00, for safety. Ja, three o'clock for sure, definite."

Last hopes of getting to the holiday cottage vanish, and I look for a bed for the night. I pick a rooming house and am rewarded by a memorable notice on the wall: "If too much noise outside, please close the window and turn on the fan." Showered, I go to settle with the landlady. She's watching TV with the sound off, and while she talks her eyes hug the box.

It's the news, and politicians are opening and closing soundless mouths. When FW[12] appears she breaks into an aside — "That old baldy! If only he had a daughter, then he wouldn't let the kaffirs on the beaches" — and goes on into a moving account of her hard times, with family rifts and domestic tragedies.

Her tale is so poignant and told with such mounting despair, especially when she comes to the present time and sons who have left and lost interest

---

12. FW de Klerk, the Sidney Carton of real life, had not yet freed the long-term prisoner whose deputy president he would later briefly be, but had recently taken to making reformist noises that shook South Africa.

in her, that eventually I feel a compulsion to change the subject.

I ask about the spookhuis. "Oh, you don't go down *there*," she says, end of subject, and turns to a lament about the paucity of business. The phone rings and she says: "Sorry. Fully booked. Nothing left. Very sorry." She hangs up, says: "Coolies,"[13] and returns to her lament.

---

13. *Impolite reference to South Africans of Indian extraction, who are becoming the nation's gentry.*

Thursday

EARLY MORNING. A WALK AROUND TOWN, I PASS A GARAGE forecourt. A combi taxi[14] is blocking a petrol tanker. A white guy screams at the driver: "Get that fucken' taxi out the way!"

The driver says the taxi's stuck. The guy yells: "Shit! There's a hundred kaffirs sitting inside there. Let them push!"

The driver says: "What do you mean by kaffirs?" (If that is a fair translation of: "Watse ding is 'n kaffer?")

The white guy looks like he's going to burst. He shoves his face at the driver in a spit-spraying bellow: "You're a kaffir! You! You!" For a moment the driver seems about to take a stand. But then he crumples and starts pushing, while his passengers sit.

Loving thy neighbour comes hard, at times. But what else? This guy's certain that if he doesn't keep the blacks small, they're going to make him small. Liberate him, to see a future, before you judge him.

The centre of action in Beaufort West is the Snoepie[15] Amusement

---

14. *Combi taxi = black taxi — fixed fare, fixed route, hugely overladen — as opposed to meter or Western taxi.*

15. *Afrikanerised version of Charlie Brown's dog.*

Arcade, where a blonde girl of no more than 12 is in charge. Thirty or more patrons, boys and young men, are playing pool and pinball and coin soccer games. They are astonishingly intermingled, white and coloured. It's not just a matter of white teams playing coloured teams, but the teams themselves are colour-blind. These kids can't be growing up like their parents did.

Then a white boy tells me about rugby and how his school plays everybody, touring the whole Karoo and even across the Langeberg. I ask if they also play the coloured school here in town, and he is scandalised.

For that matter, even the race-freeness of Snoepie's is only half-way race-free. There are no blacks. Each time I cross the Orange River it strikes me anew that we have a split set of racial conventions. In the north half of the country, the basic social distance is between whites and the rest. In the south, you have a three-stage division where the coloured-to-black gulf is as large as white-to-coloured.

I call in at a hostelry, empty but for the barman, white. He finds I am from Johannesburg and pronounces: "Well you can do what you want up there, but apartheid is never going to end, nooit."[16]

That message delivered, he settles in to a comic and says no more, so when my glass is dry I go up the road to the next hotel, where the coloured barman and coloured patrons are patently pleased to receive an unexpected white guest and are all keen philosophers. After a long analysis of South African versus South West beer qualities,[17] politics comes up.

"Apartheid?" says one guy. "It's finished here in Beaufort. Everyone can

----

16. A resoundingly categorical Afrikaans way of double-nevering the end of a sentence.

17. Little Namibia — well, sizeable but empty Namibia, with the world's second sparsest population after Mongolia, at four per square mile — has a Mighty Mouse brewery which constantly tweaks the tale of big brother across the border. Namibia is still "South West" to the kind of South Africans who connoisseur these matters.

go anywhere now. Except the bantus,[18] of course."

Indeed, one sees remarkably few blacks around town. After a bite of lunch — conversation having progressed to the distinction between ales and lagers — I say I'll go and look at the black township. Jaws drop all round, clearly signifying: Ag, no, this whitey is a weirdo.

The township is ten minutes' walk and marked by a signpost, Sidesaviwa. You can see part of it from the main road, the run-down part. The smart new part is out of sight — oddly, given the national habit of putting the fancy bits up front where tourists see them. Maybe that would have meant too close to town.

On the way, a group of kids approach me for the usual: Cigarettes and/or 20c. They look as black as anybody, and it's a surprise when they start badmouthing the blacks. Everything's fine in Beaufort, they tell me, except for the blacks. "Die Bantoes is nie[19] lekker nie." Also the blacks don't like to speak to them in Afrikaans; they want to speak English or Bantoetaal.

In the township, the first few people who try to adopt an inexplicable white pedestrian are drunk. Then there's one James, fortyish and a total gentleman. He lost his job in Springs[20] in January 1987 and came back to the bosom of the extended family, and here he waits "for my ship to come in." He might have chosen a happier metaphor, in a township without even a puddle to float a matchbox, but James's spirit is strong. He shows me the old quarter, falling to pieces, and the new, electrified and paved, and tells me this is a fine arrangement: "The people on the old side like the old side and the people on the new side like the new side."

----

18. *Abantu means "people" in the Nguni languages, of which there are about five in SA. "Bantu" was one of the various successive terms which the old white government christened Africans, or "black blacks" as opposed to half-blacks, all of which became very out and Politically Anti-correct.*

19. *"Are not nice."*

20. *An industrial town 700 miles away.*

James takes a laid-back view all round. I say I must be eating into his time, and he replies: "I'd just be sitting, otherwise." He introduces me to nearly everyone sober enough to see straight, which is about half the population. Workers being at work, we meet mainly the jobless, who all say the same: No jobs for blacks, the coloureds get the jobs. A Ciskei[21] schoolteacher, home on leave, says: "What you in the cities don't realise is that Verwoerd[22] has won. There's nothing for a black man between here and the homelands. Even petrol-boys[23] have been pushed out by coloured women."

One guy has just had a six-day job, building. He says he earned R30. I'm sceptical. James says, no, R5 a day is normal.

On local politics, he explains there are two factions: the bloupakke — police auxiliaries — are "for the whites" and the comrades are "for zabalaza" — liberation or revolution. He takes no view on who's right and who's wrong, but twice we come across bloupakke[24] in royal-blue fatigues, rifles in hand and cartridge belts on waist, and he does not greet them.

The township is full of fading zabalaza slogans, on walls and the backs of billboards. "COSUMER'S BOYOTT!" says one, evidently scrawled in haste. "STAY AWAY FROM TOWN" another; "CONSUMERS SUPPORT ZABALAZA" and more of the same.

Odd that the revolutionaries never got "zabalaza" into the world's lexicon, like the Palestinians did with "intifada." Not that De Klerk is doing any better, word-wise. "Reform" is pallid next to "perestroika" and "glasnost."

----

21. Allegedly sovereign ethnic "homeland" state in the Eastern Cape. Disappeared at the Mandela election
22. Prime Minister Hendrik Verwoerd, assassinated in 1966, was the architect of apartheid, the attempt to structurally separate the destinies of races.
23. City sensitivities would assume a Xhosa teacher to be one of first to hit the roof at an olden-days reference to adult blacks as "boys."
24. Blue overalls.

Gorbachev's PR people gave him double punch — two triggers of international imagination, while "apartheid" clings on as South Africa's sole semantic handle. Unless FW produces a label soon, the other side might yet get "zabalaza" on the map. It even has just the right ring — new and foreign, but easy for TV anchormen to pronounce.

James is vague about why the boycott took place or what it achieved. He says we should ask the organisers and leads me to a house in the old quarter where a dozen people are congregated.

Some are drunk. Some are playing cards in one of the house's two rooms. Outside, next to a malodorous toilet, a woman of about 35 is sitting on an upturned barrel chewing at two lamb chops, one in each hand. She is the captain of the team and is at first unimpressed at having her lunch invaded.

A sharp exchange, three part Xhosa to one part English, apparently ends with James reading her the riot act regarding hospitality to visitors.

She thaws and asks what I want to know. I say I want to know how it's going here in Sidesaviwa. This is a big mistake. James has told me that Sidesaviwa is a new name and that it means "At Last They Listen To Us." What he hasn't told me is that the word is a hot potato. To the comrades it's a sellout name, aimed at deluding the blacks. They use another name, Mandlenkosi,[25] in honour of a martyr killed by bloupakke on New Year's Day 1988.

Later, James amplifies: To talk of Sidesaviwa in comrade company is enemy talk, while you don't talk of Mandlenkosi when the Boers are around. I say this requires fast thinking from the man in the street. James says: "Not so much, really. Actually everybody calls the place Lokasie."[26]

----

25. *"Power of the Lord" — a common forename, usually abbreviated to Mandla — power.*

26. *"Location" — the antiquated and un-PC term for places where blacks had to live. Already long ago replaced by "township," which remains the most ☞*

My blunder settled, we discuss. Young men sprawl on boxes and rough stools and act as the woman's chorus whenever she takes time to gnaw at the corners of her lamb chops, which she finishes so cleanly there's nothing but smell for the mongrels at her feet. A drunk totters up to me, but the woman lets rip with a burst of Xhosa ack-ack and he skulks off. James and I are left standing, while everyone else is seated. I hope with fervour but in vain that someone will suggest a move upwind from the toilet. Barring the absence of grass or plants, we might as well be among Soweto's comrades: Same words, same English, same views, except for the grouch about coloureds and jobs.

South Africa lacks the normal symbols of national unity, like flag and anthem,[27] but we at least have a slogan that applies all round. It is: "I Am Not A Racist But ..."

In town, a white woman has said there's no work for whites. "The bosses in Johannesburg tell their managers: 'We're against apartheid so you must employ non-whites.' Then they pay them less so they get more profits." Two coloureds have told me there's no work for coloureds: "The Boers like the blacks because they'll work for slave wages." Now I'm told there's no work for blacks: "The Boers take coloureds, who speak their language and won't stand up for workers' rights."

"I'm not a racist," says a young man with The Struggle Lives on his

---

(26 CONTINUED) *respectable term available. Some (invariably white) ultra-PCers are trying to establish "suburb," but this causes huge miscommunication among blacks to whom "suburb" is unequivocally the white residential area to which you aspire to move when you get rich.*

27. *We do have a common flag now; the most conspicuous success of the new society. Everybody loves it. Anthem? Nearly, but not quite. The official anthem is a melding of the old black one and the old white one. Generally the whites have embraced it pretty well, even if they tend to hum through the tricky bits like "maluphakamis'uphondolwayo," but there's a growing black tendency to stop the tape before the "white" half starts.*

chest, "but these coloureds should be fair. They send their women to take our fathers' jobs, even their children. They can have three, four, wage-earners in one house! It should rather be 50/50 — when a coloured gets a job, a black man gets the next."

I'm firmly told there was total solidarity in the boycott, and no intimidation. Beyond that, the causes and consequences remain a mystery. All that is clear is that the boycott had as much to do with "the national demand" as with "local matters."

"We even marched on the town. That was Beaufort West's biggest day, and completely peaceful. We were just sorry the media weren't there. We said: 'Tell your De Klerk we are not interested in reforms and smiles. We want one-man, one-vote, that's all.' We want peace, for the whites too. We don't say Mandela is better than De Klerk, we just want that the people can choose. Peace, and correction of wrongs. Here we have six people in one shack. In town you can have two people in a six-room house. Correction must take place."

It's well after three when I return to town and the workshop, where the car is on the pit. The mechanic is out and I am received by his labourer, Thomson.

Thomson is large and humble and has a smile like sunshine. Last time round, I saw him signing for his pay packet. He signs his name "X." He seems to me to work like ten men — changing tyres and lugging parts and finding tools. Thomson doesn't know why the car is still on the pit. What he does know is the source of the original problem. He takes me to a pile of discarded parts and shows where a balancing shaft has gouged a groove in the block. He's explaining this in an enthusiastic, if baffling, jumble of little English and less Afrikaans, when suddenly he falls silent in midstream and stands up.

The mechanic has returned and fails to appreciate Thomson doing the talking. He glowers at Thomson. Thomson slinks back to work and the mechanic takes up the tale: Blame your balancing shaft.

I do not know it at the time, but this is a refrain. Over the next few weeks half the garagemen of the Karoo are about to meet this vehicle, and all of them going to say: "Mitsubishi? Must be a balance shaft." To people in the know, the concept of Mitsubishi and the concept of balance shaft problems go together like Christmas and crackers. I become a touch indignant. There's a whole industry of automobile journalism, full of acceleration times and drag coefficients. But if anyone's telling us things we need to know, like what parts to expect to pack in, they're not telling us very loud. It's not only cars, either. I bought my child a camera so bad you could confuse a family picnic for a herd of impala. When I tackled the agent, he said: "Off the record, this model is terrible." But he sells it; we let him.

Now the new balance shaft is working but the new oil pump is not. The mechanic is getting ratty, which means tough times for Thomson, who is scurrying between pit and toolbox with a river of sweat soaking his overalls and a river of abuse slamming his ears.

The workshop is thick with human traffic, including a black man in a suit and tie, brandishing banknotes. He is full of praise because the garage helped him out on trust, when he had no cash, and now he's come to pay. While he waits for the cashier, we talk. I say I've heard Beaufort West had an intimidation-free boycott.

He laughs wryly: "Yes, they didn't necklace[28] anybody. They just burnt tyres and paraffin in front of our houses."

He's about to say more, but the cashier is suddenly free and he takes his chance. He's caught the cashier's attention when a white customer — a regular, on first names — appears. The black man simply disappears from the cashier's field of vision. He steps back and waits again. When the cashier

---

28. *The awfullest single feature of the revolutionary era — the habit of squeezing old tyres around informers (or maybe-informers, or perhaps-maybe-informers, or somebody that somebody didn't like), dousing them with paraffin and applying a match. Now — cross your fingers — either a deceased practice or a dormant one.*

finally deals with him there is cheerful courtesy on both sides.

While I watch the oil pump's progress, there's a commotion at the door. It is one of the comrades.

In the township he was wearing a Struggle shirt. Now his shirt is rolled up to obscure the slogan, and he has a hand across his chest as if in urgent need to scratch an armpit. Even so, he is definitely not the kind of person who is tacitly entitled to ignore the "Private" sign. He is being glared at in shock, and he feels the chill. He sees me, blurts, "Can·I·speak·to·you·please·I·will·wait·outside," and is off.

I follow a moment later, sensing eyes on my back. He's nowhere in sight, but then I see an urgent waving from a distance.

He wants a lift. He wants to pay. "I can't use the train," he explains. "We're boycotting."

I say I'll find him in the township when the car's ready. He's still holding his arm in urgent·scratch mode. I say: "Why are you hiding your shirt? There are many people around with zabalaza shirts."

He looks sheepish, and defends himself: "They don't know what it is. When the whiteman[29] challenges, they say, 'Somebody gave it to me, baas.'"

He unrolls his shirt anyway.

It's into overtime when the car is ready for a test drive. The mechanic takes the wheel and I the passenger seat. He talks as we drive. He talks of his worries: When they build a bypass, Beaufort will die. He talks of his joys: His daughter has found a good job at a hotel near town. Inbetween he frequently mentions the two big threats: (1) Hotnots,[30] (2) Kaffers.

----

29. *Yeah, I know you expect it to be two words, but this is how blacks usually write it. Frequently they'd have a capital, too, which I can't bring myself to follow. I've liked to think of white and black as adjectives like tall or wide or young or old. In the old days it was mainly the white right which capitalised them as if to make them separate species. These days the black newspapers virtually all say Black.*
30. *Intentionally offensive term for coloured people, from Hottentot.*

It comes up that his daughter travels to work in a coloured taxi, the only white passenger. Suddenly I'm no longer hearing "Hotnot" but "Kleurling,"[31] and I'm no longer hearing threat.

Does it trouble him, her driving with coloureds?

"No ways, man. Her colleagues are very respectable people."

We're on the national road. A truck is turning right, at a point where several people are hitching. Women and children and piles of baggage are huddled in a patch of scrubby shade off the roadside. Menfolk are up in the glare at the edge of the tarmac, fingers pointed skyward, taxi-style. The truck is blocking the main lane, so no problem, we hug the left, crossing deep into the emergency lane and sending the hitchhikers scuttling for their lives.

When I get my breath back, I yell: "How could you do that!?"

"What?" he says, mystified.

"You nearly hit those people! You gave them heart failure." He thinks for a while and says: "They shouldn't be on the road. They've no right." Then he falls sullenly silent until we get back at the garage.

The car is fine.

I make out a cheque to give me heart failure of my own, and head for the township.

The number of drunks has swelled as day has drawn on, but the core knot of comrades is still bright-eyed. The lift-seeker, Paul, has gone to a "strategy meeting," leaving word to expect me. Two young men pile in to guide me, and a drunk stumbles after them. I feel reluctantly constrained to pause while he gropes for the door handle. One of his friends leans out and deals him a clout that sends him sprawling in the dust.

There is not exactly a road; just spaces of varied breadth. One minute you're in a narrow lane; the next, the middle of a dusty piazza. You don't know who might be coming at you from what angle. The pedestrians also don't know what's road or what's not — not that it would matter — and

---

31. *Politest of the numerous words for coloured people.*

there are children all over.

The terrain is dry dust, and even at snail's pace the car turns the air into clouds. Where there's not sand there's rock and often jagged rock. We move sedately, while the comrades preach. They have all the right jargon: "Institutionalised violence," "exploitation of man by man," "the majority." But they're easier to listen to than the three-piece phoneys on the diplomatic cocktail circuit, twirling the keys of sponsored Cressidas and belittling their children's Portuguese classmates between mouthing the platitudes of total change.

To these youngsters freedom is urgent. If only they could at least get past "the majority." They claim to speak for democracy and nonracialism, but see "the blacks" as "the majority" and the ANC as "the representative" of "the majority." I say: "How about black people who want to vote for De Klerk?" They are shocked. One says: "They won't be allowed to." The other, the guy who klapped the drunk, ponders longer and finally pronounces: "They won't want to."

"Why not?" I ask.

"Because they support the ANC."

"What? Everybody?"

"Yes," he says, "everybody."

There's a woman alongside, with a shopping bag in hand and a child in tow. I say: "Fine. Let's ask her."

"No, no," says the comrade hastily. "She'll become confused when she sees a white man and will deny."

He has a point there, but I stop anyway and the poor woman indeed becomes confused. She takes a nervous look, sees a white man and two blacks arguing, and scurries down the nearest lane.

Back at Union, South Africa had about twice as many blacks as whites. Say there'd been another gold rush, another burst of European immigration, and that blacks had acquired pensions and security early on, so the black birthrate was about the same as the white. We would now have more whites than blacks, but the question of how to slot the blacks into politics would remain.

What then would the majority addicts have had to say? "It's okay that we blacks are excluded, because the majority rules?" Not a damn. They'd be saying: "We want rights, we are citizens."[32]

We draw up outside the strategy meeting. The comrades are about to alight, then abruptly freeze, their jaunty confidence gone. A bakkie[33] is speeding towards us, bouncing over rocks as if the devil's close behind. "Police," whisper the comrades. They seem to know.

The bakkie isn't after us. It's storming past, but the driver glimpses my white face. The bakkie judders to a halt and a wheel-spinning reverse. The occupants are two young whites in casual clothes. The passenger is dangling

---

32. *This exchange is strangely prophetic in a back-handed way. Absolutely nobody in January 1990 believed we would have a non-racial election until after decades more banging and crashing of irresistible force upon immovable rock. Four and a half years later we stood in long long queues on a warm winter's day and wept in joy and brotherhood and pride. Everybody was delighted with the perfect result — clear Mandela victory, up-to-scratch showing for the reform-bringer, De Klerk, and more crucially also for the potential wreckers, white right and Zulu right. We suspected that some creative adding-machine work in the confusion had helped along, but who cared? We happily overlooked the rather daunting racial implications. The nation voted with its skin. If you're black, and not Zulu, it's ANC. If you're not black, anybody but. Were it not for the ethnic minorities we'd be a one-party state by democratic demand. Now, another four years on, we're seeing a slightly alarming strain of minorityitis breaking out among the paler disaffecteds, at the same time as we're seeing darker ones, especially among our neighbours where liberation has had a longer innings, saying: "Can we have the whites back now, please." Is this a weird continent, or what?*

33. *Pick-up.*

a pistol. We're window to window, breathing more sand than oxygen.

"Dag,"[34] I say.

"Dag," he nods.

They wheel-spin off. The comrades revert instantly to unfrosted, and go to collect Paul. Paul has his goods in a plastic packet, ready to leave, but he'd thought I'm going north, which I'm not, so the lift falls through. He writes me his address, in Block I, Mandlenkosi.

I ask if post gets delivered, with Mandlenkosi on the envelope.

"They're not *that* bad," he says.

A short way out of Beaufort West there's the Meiringspoort[35] turnoff. Hardly an efficient route to Cape Town, but there's less haste now that there's no hope of taking in the cottage holiday, and I've never seen the poort. I take the turn. Three young blacks scramble to their feet, hands in prayer position, cries of "my kroon"[36] and "asseblief."

There's not as much as a farm-stall for a week's walk ahead of them, and I feel bad as they shrink in the mirror, my mind's ear hearing them curse my back. But it's their fault. They should be half a mile apart. One hitcher on a lonely road, I'll pick up. Three at a time, no. More than a classroom, what these guys need is a kick in the posterior, like the freelance parking attendants who give you the same frustration. Nobody needs ushering into a parking bay. What you need is change for the meter. Here's the opening for the parking consultants, but nine out of ten screw it up.

The Meiringspoort road is straight and empty, the Swartberg rising through the evening. Farms like the Trekkers thought farms should be, where

---

34. *Rhymes with Bach. Means "G'Day." I guess you guessed.*
35. *Poort — the dictionary says "gate or entrance," which is pretty poor. Rather a path through a mountain range, for which North America of all places must have plenty of words.*
36. *"My king," a really badly brown-nose fashion by which some blacks address whites or coloureds when in need. Asseblief is "please."*

you can't see the smoke of the neighbour's chimney. Nothing on the road but tortoises.

The car develops an automatic window. Wind it up, and it automatically falls down. But who needs windows in a Karoo summer? The Swartberg looms ever larger until it is no longer a horizon but a towering bulk.

There's water, all of a sudden. Water!

Water, and then there's grass and green things and visibility is cut from forever to zero. Zero horizontally, anyhow, with rockface either side. Now you can look *up* forever, like an insect from the base of a high narrow box. A fairytale stream meanders through the kloof, and round each corner there's another stretch of poort. Ten times or twenty I think this must be the end. Ten times or twenty I am wrong. Meiringspoort goes on and on, and you can marvel that Mr Meiring ever worked his way through this mighty gateway of God. I stop to walk, and the vastness puts man in his puny place.

The pools are small, though sparkling. I'm watching for the right place to swim. Then there's a surprise sign — "Waterfall."

The fall is slim but stately, enclosed on three sides by cliffs to heaven, soaring so lofty that the royal blue of the closing evening is but an eye over the roundest deepest coldest rock pool ever. The road is out of sight and earshot. Hawks and eagles circle in silhouette above the eerie echoes of unseen baboons. The right place to swim.

On to De Rust, whose single street is a promenade. Pedestrians are strolling and greeting, drifting through the speckled streetlight, calling out to householders on stoeps. I park the car and join the perambulators.

Villagers are clustered at the general dealer's steps and perplexed at a stranger on foot. They enquire, and I'm required to offer "the Johannesburg perspective" on everything from Gorbachev to the ozone layer.

The callbox — working![37] — informs my family, 300 miles ahead, that

---

37. *A considerably rarer experience in Africa than, I suspect, in Canada.*

all is fine, very fine. I'll drive awhile, sleep till daybreak, back for morning tea. Even in the dark the Little Karoo, this side of the mountain, is different to the Great — trees and ostriches and grass. "The Little Karoo," a Beaufort West boy had said scornfully, "is not even half a desert."

Here the arid majesty is less arid and thereby arguably less majestic, but the vegetation is a relief. The Great Karoo and its adjuncts — Doring Karoo, Upper Karoo, Southern Kalahari — are already the size of France and still spreading. That's enough arid majesty.

The road is quiet, the car is purring, the air is crisp. An astonishing white light appears behind the berg, framing it so vividly that for a bewildered moment I wonder whether this is the Second Coming or nuclear war. Then the head of a full moon peeks reassuringly over the edge, and within minutes it's so bright you could lose your headlights and keep the road.

A settlement in the distance. Dysselsdorp, says the map, and I guess this is one of the Cape's coloured towns.

The Cape, unlike the rest of the country, did not just shove everyone of colour in a township and have done. It also has coloured hamlets, built around mission stations, with space and grace and cohesion and old-time rustic beauty that will one day send tourist boards orgasmic, but so far with nothing by way of an economy, like hotels.

But there must be a shebeen.[38] My stomach is starting to grumble, and I look out for the turnoff.

Graaaaaaaak.

A sound I know. I heard it 40 miles from Beaufort West. The red dashboard lights spring to life; the engine falls silent. I can't believe it.

---

38. *An unlicensed bar, usually African but sometimes coloured. They're less illegal now than they used to be, so the top topic is nostalgia for the good old days when the Boer police used to bust in and break bottles and/or heads. The word was originally Irish, but is there now obsolete, I believe.*

It's many minutes till a vehicle appears, a tiny bakkie from which a burly man emerges to offer tools and a torch. But we'd need a block and tackle.

There's nothing in Dysselsdorp, he says. He'll take me to Oudtshoorn[39] but first we must get someone to watch the car.

That's crazy, I think. There's no-one around, and if there were, why should they care, or we trust them? The man, Toby, looks at me sharply. "They're Coloured people," he says, the capital C tall in his voice. I realise then that he is coloured, too.

Toby bellows into the night like a foghorn. "HAAI! WIE'S DAAR? HULLOOO!"

After some time figures loom through the moonlight. "This combi is from Johannesburg," says Toby, conferring guest status upon it. "Keep watch, hoor."

The dim figures nod.

The cab is carrying Toby's wife and two children. I say I'll ride in the back but he won't hear of it. So there are ten knees in a space meant for four, and that he manages to change gear is a miracle. On the short drive to Oudtshoorn, Toby and Mrs Toby outline their philosophy of life — God is readying us for an Age of Beauty about to dawn — and debate in detail where to drop me, assessing rival hotels from which until recently they were barred by law. They decide on the Queens Hotel, insist on waiting until I'm checked in, and extract a promise that I'll phone if in need.

The hotel kitchen re-opens to oblige a latecomer, and then I phone Thinus, the garage boss in Beaufort West. I don't expect much. He has his money.

Thinus is asleep. When it registers that his garage's repair job has lasted less than half a day, he is mortified.

---

39. *One-time ostrich capital of the world. Still a regional capital, but a tad run-down now that our former ostrich hegemony has been diffused.*

"Leave it to me," he says. "I'll make a plan." That'll be the day, I think as I hang up. But the hassles and haggling can wait till morning.

Friday

AT BREAKFAST I GET A CALL FROM AN OUDTSHOORN GARAGE:
"We've towed your car in and stripped it. We're handling it top speed — we
owe Thinus some favours. Thinus says to charge everything to him and to fill
your petrol tank. The parts are in stock. Come up in an hour and you can take
it away."

They're wrong, of course, but only by a few hours — hours I spend
watching the workshop. This is a pleasure, as the garage is a model of what the
"New South Africa" is meant to be — harmony and all-round respect, except I
don't know how "new" this is because everybody seems well worn in.

By midday we're in business. We start the car and rev it and test it and
stop it and start it again and do it all over. Good as new. I phone Thinus with
thanks, and am ready to go. Farewells all round, and no raised eyebrows when
I shake hands with the blacks. The manager and mechanics and labourers gather
at the car like hoteliers seeing a prize guest off, and I turn the key and there's
nothing.

Nothing happens. The starter's packed in. Just like that. No-one can
believe it. They're wondering, could this be Funny People or what? But they
get behind and push. The engine roars and I hightail it out of town.

43

The drive through the Little Karoo is peace and calm, marked by humble dorps and humble hitchhikers and the beautiful ageing mansions of ostrich barons, but a nagging vision is growing in my mind: The vision of my family's faces when I arrive in Cape Town to load them up.

"Hooray, daddy's here!"

"Hi guys. All's well. We'll leave for Jo'burg tonight."

"Er... where's the car?"

"Oh, on the hill. It's fine, really, if you have a hill to start it on."

By the time I get to Cape Town the workshops will be shut for the weekend, so at Swellendam I hunt up the Mitsubishi agent on the offchance. Yep, says the foreman, this starter's far gone. Nope, there is none in stock. But not to worry, it so happens that Swellendam is the seat of the best starter specialist south of the equator. "You'll be on the road in an hour." I seem to have heard this before, but in five minutes time the starter is tucked under my arm, wrapped in newspaper, and in another five the foreman is dropping me off, from his bakkie, at the starter shop.

The starter shop proclaims "WE DO ONLY ONE THING AND WE DO IT VERY WELL." It is run by a German and a coloured, both named Frans, who explain the secret of their success: Ignore parts numbers. There are thousands of starter models. One that looks right in the parts directory might be a vital millimetre out when it's under the spanner. Or one that the vehicle manufacturer never heard of might fit like a glove when you match it to the engine.

So you don't read directory numbers to the Franses. You bring in the real thing. The Franses pick it up, turn it round, hold it up, hold it down, hold it sideways, pass it between each other, furrow their brows, and brainstorm. They have a vast reconditioned stock and try to think of a compatible unit, talking of each individual starter as if it's an old friend. "Perhaps that one near the end of the second shelf," says one Frans. "I think its diameter's too wide," says the other, "but at the back, on the top ..."

"Ah yes!" says Frans, clicking his fingers, and they're off to inspect. But they're out of luck. The perfect fit is not to be had, so the Franses start to cannibalise. Armatures and brushes and casings and endplates are matched and re-matched until the pile on the bench looks like experimental sculpture.

My starter is obstinate, and it's becoming a point of pride to get it right. The Franses pay less and less notice to the distraction of incoming customers. The shop fills up with farmers and mechanics and messengers, clutching grimy starter motors and chatting.

A mechanic tells me with damp-eyed sincerity about Christ's will for South Africa, part of which is: "Since we Afrikaners[40] have messed it up, now we're meant to give it to the blacks." Two young guys in overalls — one white, one coloured — have their heads together in terrifically deep discussion. A hearty coloured in a safari suit is telling loud dirty jokes. A

---

40. *"Afrikaner," which obviously means nothing but "African" in Afrikaans, is applied to white people who speak a language mainly descended from Dutch. It is widely but wrongly assumed that Afrikaners mainly came from Holland. Actually more than half are of French origin. Their forebears emigrated when the Revocation of the Edict of Nantes in 1685 said it was once again okay to beat up Protestants. Somehow they lost their language so totally that barely a French inflexion is left. A Mr Labuschagne, pronounced La-boo-skacgh-knee, might go to a rest-too-rahndt to order a fillitt-michnorn. There are also plenty of Afrikaners with Portuguese ancestry, notably Ferreiras, plus Spanish, Polish and Italian. There are English such as Smith pronounced Smit or Coombe pronounced Koem-bie, who mainly got there by love and marriage, and Irish such as O'Connell, pronounced O'Connell, who partly got there because there were nice opportunities to fight the English. "Boer" and "Afrikaner" can be used pretty much interchangeably, as I use them here. However, "Afrikaner" is an entirely neutral term, safely employed by anybody any time any place, whereas "Boer" (which technically means nothing but the innocuous "farmer") carries a huge portmanteau of hidden subtleties. It can connote anything from contempt to deference depending on context, and can lead into historical and political ☛*

45

heterogenous group has formed round a dice game at the end of the passage.

When either Frans lifts his eyes from my starter, there's instant lull. The Franses are kings here, everybody wanting their attention. I got in at an opportune moment, and the crowds must wait until finally I am proudly presented with what one Frans calls the most bastard starter he ever saw, with portions of Ford and Toyota and Massey-Ferguson in its ancestry.

It's a moment's work for the garage to refit the starter to the car, and by dusk I'm pointed to Cape Town. "That's not quite the hour you promised," I say to the foreman. He laughs: "You knew what I meant."

Outside Swellendam I pick up a young coloured factory worker who makes up in wit what he lacks in schooling. He's explaining how to tell when someone's going to die, by learning to read the portents, when we come to Riviersonderend. "If Meneer would like to stop for a minute," he says, "I'd like to buy Meneer a cooldrink." I stop at a cafe and he comes back with ginger beer, which is a smart investment.

Where he's going — Harmony Park, a coloured township near Somerset West — is a few miles off my route. I could take him there or I could leave him to walk the last stretch, and he astutely figures that if he injects a contribution into the relationship I am more likely to do the former. I wish he could go out and educate the average benighted hitchhiker, who silently worries himself silly throughout the ride and then at the end, when you drop him, holds out a pathetic collection of grubby notes and asks how much he must pay.

(40 CONTINUED) *minefields. Some Boers refuse to recognise other Boers as Boers, and some Afrikaners won't recognise any Boers at all. Thus, not advised for passing visitors. Meantime in English "Africans" are by no means "Afrikaners." Africans are the indigenous full-scale blacks. Thus the half-blacks whose home (and often only) language is Afrikaans are neither "Afrikaners" nor "Africans." And there you have it. It's simple when you get the hang of it, like the rules of cricket.*

When we get to Harmony Park the coloured guy is telling me about nomenclature. This thing about "bruinmense"[41] is bad news, he says. "We're Coloureds, Kleurlinge, that's what we should be called, not 'bruinmense.'" He spits the word out in disgust.

I say I've heard that some coloured people like to be called "black." He mistakes my meaning. "No," he says, "the blacks are over there, in Lwandle." He points to the African township in the distance.

I say I mean people who are classified "coloured" but consider themselves "black." He looks puzzled. "No" he says, "I never heard of that."[42]

It's well into dark when I rejoin my family and impractical to leave for Johannesburg tonight, as scheduled. Oh well, hardly an imposition. We take a last Saturday of Cape sun and sea.

---

41. *Brown people. Bernard Shaw in Pygmalion says: "the moment an Englishman opens his mouth another Englishman despises him." In South Africa it happens the moment you refer to an ethnic group. This word is meant to be super-polite, mainly used by the kind of people who say "lavatory" or "persons."*

42. *Eight years later, he must have. In the early nineties it became such a hugely in-thing among coloured intellectuals to be "black" that the echoes must have rung through Harmony Park. However, it is now the late nineties, and the wheel of history has taken another of its endlessly cussed lurches. The intellectual fashion has tilted sharply in the direction of revolting against a world perpetually divided into "black" and "white" (a tilt with which I for one am in deep sympathy). The streetside fashion has taken a different tilt, presenting to the black brothers a more blatant raving in-your-face racism than you'll find in almost any corner of white society.*

Week Three

ON SATURDAY EVENING, WHEN WE START TO LOAD THE CAR
for midnight departure, there's petrol running down the drive. Out of the
blue, we've sprung a leak. The grandparents' village network is again put to
work. On Sunday morning a tolerant garage proprietor rousts a mechanic and
opens his workshop, and by lunchtime we're on our way.

We skim through the Boland, vines and old oak and fertility, and the
Hex River Valley, idyllic amid the spectacular protection of its enfolding
crags, and it feels almost like a home-coming as we emerge from the pass into
the familiar serene vastness of the Great Karoo. There's singing in the car,
from tape or occupants or both. There are card games and word games and
wrestles and hugs on the bunk-bed at the back. The sun-roof is open. The sky
is big, the Karoo is reassuring and restful, the road is wide and good; the
world is alright.

We stop to refuel at the first town, Laingsburg. We stretch legs,
patronise the invaluable local ice-cube industry, get back in the car, switch on,
and move six inches.

Graaaaaaak.

A farmer is filling his bakkie at the next pump. He strolls over. "Got a problem?" he asks, leisurely. Detail seems superfluous. I reply: "When's the Trans-Karoo?" He glances at his watch, and is suddenly as galvanised as Clark Kent in a phone booth. "Now!" he says. "Let's go!"

We and the farmer and the petrol-jockeys and the hangers-around clear the combi at fire-rescue speed, piling goods in a dishevelled heap in the back of the bakkie. The farmer treats Laingsburg's main road like a hotrod track and we hit the station in the nick of time. A coloured guy in railway uniform joins the dash to bring the baggage from the bakkie, and curtly commands an Afrikaans family on the platform, greeting an arriving relative, to help too. The train starts moving just as the puffing father and his two sons shove the last of our blankets and pillows through the window.

We lean out of the window, chests heaving and sweat pouring. It's too late to get names and addresses. We wave thanks to the improbable crew on the platform. They wave back till we're out of sight, like people seeing cousins off on a long far trip.

The corridor looks like a disaster-relief depot. By luck, the conductor has a vacant compartment right where we are, and then for the second time in barely more than a fortnight I find myself in a conversation I can't understand.

We don't have enough cash for the fare, and the conductor is being extremely accommodating about finding ways round this small problem. I'd like to think he's just a nice guy, but I'm again left wondering how much of its due revenues the Railways receives.

The Railways, one is told, is an institution in decay — and indeed that is not all wrong. The ancient stations have curves in their roofs and curlicues in their trellises; the modern ones are starkly functional. Where there were once handsome benches of wood and wrought-iron, there are now ugly lumps of modular grey plastic.

At De Aar, the old bar is boarded up. The "Whites Only" sign is still there, faded and irrelevant, and the noble teak counter, I imagine, is either left to the termites or gone for firewood. The new bar is abuzz with life, the whites as integral as the rest, but physically it's a blank and barren room with not a hint of elegance. Why we can't have the teak as well as the good vibe, I don't know.

On the whole, though, decline is far from evident as the Trans-Karoo thunders through the heart of the country. The dining car, for instance, is as ornate as ever. Same starched white tablecloths, same solid weightlifter cutlery, same uniformed waiters with Victorian tunics and polished buttons. It's a la carte now — you no longer have soup automatically slapped in front of you with barrowloads of starch to follow — but still strong on civil-service rigidity. Coffee with all items except No 9, the menu specifies; two slices of bread with all except 1, 2, and 9.

The staff set-up seems as traditional as ever, too: Wholly male and colour-coded. Whites serve the meals, coloureds produce the bedding, and blacks don't work on the train at all.

However, late at night I make my way down swaying corridors to the front of the train, the non-white end, and am surprised by the scene in the dining car, which is the borderline. The staff are off duty, relaxing in the seats. The formality of earlier has disappeared, and so has the segregation.

The train is full, mainly at taxpayers' expense. Half the passengers are army — a changed army to the one I knew in call-up days. We'd never have dared be seen in uniform trousers and bare chests, or in sandals and T-shirts with rifles over our backs. The other half are largely railmen on transfer, railmen on holiday, retired railmen, and railmen's dependents.

When we ask youngsters about their career intentions, they simply tell us which branch of railway work they have in mind. We acquire a sense of the railways as a total subculture, providing its own customers and breeding its own continuity.

Tik-a-tik, tik-a-tik. Every door is open, every window too, the train turning hot Karoo air into a cool breeze. Children's hide-and-seeks broaden first through compartments and then through carriages. Adults talk first to neighbours, then to neighbours' neighbours and on.

Tik-a-tik, tik-a-tik. Minuscule stations come and go, often populated by onlookers in unbelievable numbers. At Letjiesbos, for one, there is a sum total of four dwellings in the whole endless landscape, but a hundred people are sitting on the platform to watch the train come in.

At Merriman, the most picturesque station of the lot, there are many more than a hundred. A coloured woman calls to the passengers leaning out of corridor windows: "Ons het 'n mooi stasie, né?"[43] Passengers call out assent.

Then as the train starts to move, a soldier in the next carriage shouts "A.W.B."[44] and brandishes a wicked knife at the platform.

Most of the coloureds on the platform laugh. One man yells: "Ry maar, Boere."[45] Whether this is meant to be hostile, friendly or neutral, I don't know. I doubt the soldiers know, but a barrage of beercans flies at him from the vicinity of the knife.

Tik-a-tik, tik-a-tik. "And the solemn firmament marches, And the hosts of heaven arise," said Kipling of a Karoo nightfall, and he got it right. The hills looked distant by day, but in the moonlight they're the ends of the earth.

The children compete for top-bunk status, which is fine as the middle bunk puts wind on your face and a view to infinity.

Tik-a-tik, tik-a-tik. Honeymooners should travel by train.

I want to phone a friend to meet us at Park Station in Johannesburg,

----

43. *We have a pretty station, hey? (Eight years later it's an ex-station, disused and vandalised to smithereens.)*
44. *Afrikaner Weerstands Beweging — Afrikaner Resistance Movement — then a fearsome pseudo-Nazi gang with hopes of staging a Fascist putsch. Currently a lonely club of Rambo wannabes who could hold their a.g.m. in the bar of a village hotel. A resurgence, sad to say, is not impossible. Afrikaners, having rather extraordinarily abdicated their jackboot rule, increasingly suspect that after all the boot has merely moved to somebody else's foot.*
45. *Keep travelling, Boers.*

and at long-stop stations I explore the callboxes. At Beaufort West there's a 10-yard queue for the only working phone. (Also a locked toilet. The man at the ticket office says they unlock it just as soon as the train leaves.) De Aar is similar, and a fellow traveller says: "Jeez, these munts[46] will hog that phone all night."

At Kimberley, the callboxes are free, but 2 a.m. is not a tactful time to phone for favours. So I take a walk along the platform instead.

Initially, the platform appears empty. The south end, white first and second class, is empty. The middle, non-white first and second class, is also empty. And then it's a great surprise to suddenly bump into the third-class waiting room, which is full of sleeping people. It is a room to seat perhaps a hundred, and there are about 300 sleeping inside it — sleeping on floors, sleeping on laps and shoulders, sleeping against dustbins, sleeping against walls.

The room is brightly lit and a surreal sight. It looks like a medieval witch story, where everybody has swallowed a sleeping potion. I stare incredulously, until a sixth sense notifies me that something odd is happening further up north, where there are no lights and the ground seems to be covered by sacks.

I move northwards and realise that the sacks are people, not hundreds but thousands, covering the ground like an inert human carpet.

A solitary railway official is illuminated by a hand-lamp. I make my way over, toes feeling for concrete between the limbs. We are two white faces in the lamplight, surrounded by dead of night and a sea of black bodies.

"Is it always like this?" I whisper. He replies loud and clear: "Ag, not usually, but some of our kaffirs are on strike and these poor people suffer."

---

46. *Rude word, once again, for Africans. Derived from the perfectly respectable "umuntu," Nguni for "person," but mangled. Of course, when this guy gets to the phone, no way will he make his conversation short and snappy for the sake of the queues behind him; but when the blacks do the same it's a racial issue.*

By Klerksdorp, it's daylight. I take my coins and make for a callbox. The first is out of order. The second is out of order. A black man carrying a lunchpail comes up and says: "All this phones, broken."

"Where will I find one?"

"In town. I take you."

"The train's going to leave. Will you phone for me?"

"Write the number."

I write the number and start adding names. He stops me.

"No words, only numbers. What I must say?"

"Ask them to be at Park Station at ten o'clock."

The guard is raising his green flag. I run.

At Park Station at ten, our friend is waiting

From home, I phone Thinus in Beaufort West. He chuckles deep when I say the timing's blown again: "Ha ha. Man, that would be all we need, hey?" When he realises I mean it, he is so apologetic that I fear for the phone bill.

Thinus has the car towed the 200 kilometres from Laingsburg to his garage — "At least we're lucky it broke down so close," he says. Two days later he rings: It's fixed, definite, for sure, triple-checked.

But the car's in Beaufort West and I'm in Johannesburg and we skirt how it's going to get from there to here.

A family summit conference over supper. Legally, we feel, we can thump Thinus with railing it. But he's been good and, after all; it's our car, so Sunday evening the family is at the Greyhound bus station to bid me bon voyage.

Week Four

AFTER A THOUSAND KILOMETRES[47] ON THE BUS, MY NECK IS in knots. A bracing dawn is rising over Beaufort West. A walk along Bird Street, in the town's oldest section, loosens the knots and also transports me through a time warp. Most of the houses look like a set for a frontier movie, and where the glass in the shopfronts ripples with age, even the price-tags are from another era. You can buy a briar pipe for three rands or a second-hand bicycle for thirty.

At this hour, every pedestrian greets every other, and when an aged man on his way home from night shift sees me peering at a faded plaque, he comes over. I must notice, he tells me, that the plaque is in English only. "They were never fair to us," he says, "but we're fair to them." He takes me to another plaque, a very new one commemorating the night of 15-16 November 1989, when 124 millimetres of rain fell on the town.

"See," he says, "it's in both languages, even though there are hardly any

----

47. *We've been into kilometres for 30 years or so now, since soon after the whites voted, extremely narrowly, to break loose of Mama England. I've imperialised many measurements here for a North American publication, but patriotically cling to a few of our own. Anyway, "after 621 miles on the bus" doesn't strike the same note.*

English people left."

"So there used to be English people?"

"Yo!" he says. "We Afrikaners counted for nothing. The English ran the town and the Malays ran the businesses."

"Where are they now?"

"Some of the English left," he says, "and the rest became Afrikaans. Even now, many people in town have English surnames, although they're just as Afrikaans as the rest of us."

"And the Malays?"

He furrows his brow and thinks. Then he says: "You know, that's a good question."

He wants me to look at the war memorial, a distance off. When we arrive he says: "Now read that and tell me what's funny." The memorial pays tribute to fallen townsmen, starting with Blood River[48] in 1838. Up to World War II, the heroes' names are engraved in stone, but an additional plate has been affixed afterwards. Five names are painted on it, soldiers who have died between 1970 and last year, mainly aged 18 or 19.

This plate is what is bugging the old man. He points out that the other wars were *wars*, duly titled, duly dated. But the post-1970 section just says: "Ons Vir Jou, Suid Afrika — South Africa, Dear Land." Are we at war, or are we not? he asks. Why does the plate leave so much empty space beneath these five names? Why does nobody explain: Who are we fighting against, about what, until when?[49]

I collect the car from Thinus at sunrise. It's a beautiful day, bright and blue, a temptation to take the long way home.

----

48. *First big battle between Afrikaners and Zulus.*
49. *Good questions. For about 20 years South Africa was simultaneously an orderly sovereign state with a government (elected by 20% of the people) whose writ ran indubitably well; and also engaged in low-key war with people who thought the other 80% ought also to get a look-in.*

Part of Britain's legacy to the Cape is a series of dots around the sparsest part of the map, sounding like a House of Lords rollcall. Williston, Carnarvon, Meltonwold — aristocrats of the English empire are commemorated in bastions of the Afrikaner republic. I've never seen most of these places. Here's a chance.

Shortly out of Beaufort West there's a sign to Loxton. I swing off the N1 and take the gravel pass over the Nuweveldberg.

Half an hour on, a car is at the roadside. The occupants appeal frantically. There are three men, two women, two children, and a baby; coloured people. The car is medium sized and bears badges of battle. The doors and mudguards and boot are diverse colours beneath the rust, held in place by rope and wire. One tyre is flat. The spare is also flat, and its rim is mangled from a meeting with a rock or pavement. The battery is flat.

They have been there since yesterday afternoon. They ask for jump-leads. If they can start the car they'll go on to Beaufort. On a flat? "Ag, that's nothing baas, we'll drive slow."

We contemplate tactics, with difficulty since their brand of Afrikaans — their mother tongue — is almost a foreign language to the brand I know. What comes through clearest is that they are out of cigarettes. Also, as an afterthought, out of food. I can't oblige in the first respect. In the second I have only a few sweets, sweat-welded into a globule at the bottom of a plastic bottle. The men prise sweets into their mouths. A woman in the car shrieks with rage, and the men grudgingly pass her what's left. It transpires that she is the baby's mother and has also been sustaining the children — nephews — from her breast through the night.

Water, at least, is plentiful. They happen to have broken down next to the Sakrivier, the only running stream in hundreds of miles.

"Lucky," I remark. "God guided us," they reply.

A bakkie draws up. It carries a local farmer, one Werner. He is puzzled at a Jo'burger on the back roads of the mid Cape. I'm taking a whiff of the Karoo, I say. He says if I whiff long enough I'll be snared. He's been here all his life and wouldn't be anywhere else.

I say I've heard it's getting dryer, harsher. On the contrary, he says, it's getting wetter and greener. "We wrecked it, in the past. We used to overgraze it — as much as one sheep per hectare. But now we don't even think of more than one sheep per four hectares. The government has done fantastic work, educating the farmers. You can even see grass coming back if you look closely, and there'll be more and more because vegetation holds the water and recycles it."

Werner also runs a game farm in the Nuweveldberg[50] and a stud in its foothills. He rattles off a list of his champions, which include several of those few racehorse names that even the layest of laymen know, such as Roland's Song and Wainui.

Werner is upbeat on the Karoo's future, once the grass has returned, but the present has a sadness. "People are leaving. The small farmer, on five or ten thousand hectares,[51] can't make out any longer. You should see the abandoned farmhouses; tragic. The towns, too. Every second house is for sale and no-one is buying."

Werner's heading south, away from home. I'm heading north. It is arranged that I'll take the two men with their tyres and battered rim to Werner's farm, and the foreman, Karel, will sort them out in the farm workshop. Giving directions to his farm, Werner says: "You'll know when you get there. You can't miss it."

He's right. It is a massive vivid oasis. If you took the classiest thatched house in Sandown,[52] with the biggest trees and the greenest lawn, and wizarded it to the middle of nowhere … that's about what we have here. There's a dam, too, astonishingly — a dam you could ski on, never mind swim in — sourced from the same Sakrivier.

----

50. *All these places ending in "-berg" are mountain ranges. I'm sure you figured.*

51. *One hectare is two-and-a-bit acres.*

52. *Stockbrokersville, the old-money and big-money part of Johannesburg.*

I leave my passengers with Karel the foreman, a smart sergeant-majorly coloured who looks at them with an undisguised I-smell-excrement expression. Karel, I am fascinated to see, is bilingual in one language. He speaks to me in flawless textbook Afrikaans, as comprehensible as a newsreader, and when he turns to them he swops to their brand and I don't know what's going on.

A few miles along there's another extraordinary farmstead — much older and intriguingly eerie. I pause, tempted. Emboldened by meeting Werner, I feel I have a connection with the area. I take the turn-off. Trees encase the long straight drive like walls and a ceiling, as low as the combi's roof, and lead to the kind of house you might find on a postcard or a catalogue of national monuments.

It's closed and barred. The extensive outhouses are shut. There's not a bark or quack or chirrup. I leave the car to ogle the craftsmanship and breathe the emptiness, and nearly jump out of my skin when a voice at my right ear says: "Dag, baas."[53]

This belongs to a caretaker, of sorts, a soul entrapped in a feudal dreamworld. He says a hundred times that Baas Johnny van der Westhuizen has gone to town, Baas Johnny van der Westhuizen is coming back, Baas Johnny van der Westhuizen will restore the farm. I watch the tree-lined drive,

---

53. I think you've also figured out "Baas." It means something between "Sir" and "Squire," but is only ever said by people who aren't white to (male) people who are; and the proud stand-your-man kind of black guy would choke over the term. However a supplicant in full swing, such as when wanting to borrow money or protest innocence, can Baas you with every second word. I have known white people get extremely uptight, even to fisticuffs, if a black person addresses them as Meneer, Mister, which would be quite okay or even a little Victorian from a white stranger. Others, myself included, find Baas obnoxiously ingratiating (and know that the guy who Baases you most in your presence is also the guy who shafts you fastest in your absence). It's fading now, although breaking no speed records.

expecting the great Johnny to come barrelling up in a bakkie any moment. But it slowly emerges that he has been away for months or years, his return awaited in awful vain.

I wish the man well and slip him a note. He looks at the money without interest. I start the engine and am almost gone when he yells: "Baas! Baas!" I stop and he comes running. "Has the baas perhaps also got a cigarette?" I mentally note to keep a stock in the cubbyhole.

When I get to Loxton, my first stop is the callbox at the post office. It's a crankhandle phone. I grind until the operator comes on and I hear her voice twice — once on the phone and once through the wall. We're so close that if the bricks were to vanish we'd be in embarrassing intimacy. The sensation is bizarre.

The line to Johannesburg is blocked, and while we wait the operator provides the low-down on Loxton's eateries: Breakfast is out, the time is long gone, but if I go to the old-age home and place a down payment, at lunchtime there'll be a nutritious meal waiting.

I say I appreciate that good and Godfearing people do not eat breakfast at half past ten, but I'm not sure about hanging around till 1.00. She says: "Oh, but there's quite a lot to see."

Like what?

"Well, the main building is the primary school hostel."

Why not? I make my way to the hostel. It is indeed the main building. It also has six occupants. "But," says the matron. "There are still 14 day-children at the school."

I walk further, into an area marked by quaint houses, no people, and pears. The streets are lined with pear trees — real pear pears, not prickly pears.[54] Pears are rotting on the ground, nobody to eat them. There is no

----

54. *Prickly pears, a.k.a. Turksvy, or Turkish fig, are a kind of harsh desert vegetation euphemistically perceived as a "fruit" by the legions of people who pick them wild and try to sell them at the roadsides, at rates of 50c per bag.*

breathing thing in sight, four-footed or two-, enfranchised or dis-, motorised or pedestrian; nobody but an old man with a bad back who manoeuvres up to me, sticks out a beefy hand, and says: "Kleynhans."

Kleynhans came in 1949. He and his brother, boilermakers. "Meneer," he says, "when you look at this town now, and think of what it was, you want to crawl under a bush and cry. When we came, there wasn't a room to be had. We had to get a piece of canvas and make ourselves a tent out there on the veld. Now, if you wave five rand you can take your pick."

"How many people are there now?" I ask.

He thinks for a long while, thumbing at his fingers as he counts. "Fifty two," he says finally. "Or maybe fifty one."

"And the township?"[55]

"Oh, there. I don't know. Could be 200 or 300. Those poor people, they're worse off than us. You get one pensioner who's got to feed twenty mouths. Mind you, at least they have fun. You should hear the noise that end on a Saturday night. We don't have anything to do except go to funerals."

There are two general dealers in Loxton. The Minimark is on the Carnarvon road at one end of town, and Ben's is at the opposite end. Each thinks the other is at an unfair advantage.

"That Minimark," says Ben's, "they're near the township and they get all the business."

At the Minimark I'm told: "That Ben's, they're right away from the township so they don't get the theft."

The Minimark's speciality is smoked chicken. Ben's is more eclectic. It

----

55. Here, "township" automatically means coloured people. This deep into the Karoo there has never been a black African presence. Indeed some people here have never seen a black African at all; an unusual relationship with the people who theoretically provide 85% of the decision-making that affects your life. In a place like Loxton, also, everybody speaks Afrikaans. English is a virtually foreign language, and Xhosa might as well be, say, Inuit.

stocks hats and it stocks patent medicines to cure practically anything under the sun for between R1,50 and R2,90 a packet, and you can get a hamburger or chips if you don't mind a very long wait while the equipment warms up.

Ben's is run by a young couple from Pretoria. They came because they liked the idea of the family staying together and escaping the city rush, and they still like the idea but now in the abstract more than the concrete. They're going broke, because "Loxton's farmers have no loyalty. Instead of supporting their own, they just go off to Carnarvon where there are plenty of shops, twelve or thirteen. They don't even care that Carnarvon's been taken over by a Coolie."

The Indraf Kafee[56] next door has closed. You can see its crocheted tablecloths and hand-written menu through the windows. Ben's is next in line, and shortly Mr Kleynhans is going to tick fewer fingers for his tally.

On the Carnarvon road I pick up a hitchhiker. From a distance I think he's a child wrapped in a blanket. Close up, I find a coloured man barely more than four foot tall, dressed in an outsize black serge suit which must feel like a sauna from within. His features are more classically bushman[57] than anybody I've ever seen in real life, and he calls me by a word I've never heard. It sounds like "duisman" and he uses it about ten times per sentence. Then he tells me he used to think Upington was the biggest town in the world, but now he's just been to Port Elizabeth so he knows better. He's on his way home, and has been five days on the road. I work out that he's nearly half way, with the busy parts behind him and the empty parts ahead, and I

----

56. *"Come-in Cafe."*

57. *Bushmen and Hottentots, the truly native South Africans, form two of the strands of heritage of today's coloured people, along with Malays, Indians and a zillion varieties of ethnic intermarriage. The number of card-carrying actual Bushmen, who speak the original language which is now written in a hieroglyphic series of inverted exclamation-marks, can't be more than a few hundred. They're mainly in places where you pay ten rand to go and take ☛*

estimate that at this rate he'll take about as long to cross the Cape as Phineas Fogg did to cross a hemisphere. He spends most of the time bragging about the greatness and goodness of his employer, who was once the mayor of Aggeneys, and I think I'd love to hear the comrades try to tell this guy that he won't be allowed to vote for the Boere.

Carnarvon at midday is ashimmer with heat. It has a large and tantalising swimming pool, locked. The pool closes for the four hottest hours, working on a similar principle to museums that close on weekends and post offices that close at lunch. But at least there's a bar, quite some bar. It is lined with thousands of beer cans from around the globe; decorated with a startling variety of pictures of copulation, human, animal, or a bit of both; and run by an English lady who speaks like a character out of PG Wodehouse. People address her in Karoo Afrikaans — Tannie Di,[58] they call her — and she replies in Eton English. Everybody seems accustomed to this procedure, and I ask Tannie Di how long she's been in Carnarvon.

Since 1955, she says, and since then she's been assembling a unique collection of rare whiskys. "There might be bigger collections in America or somewhere, but none have got this." She forages in the cabinet and produces

----

(57 CONTINUED) *pictures. There are hundreds of thousands of Bushmanish-looking coloured people, though, speaking Afrikaans and wearing clothes. It is a common offensive practice for white people or black people to call coloureds "Boesman," but plenty of coloureds will happily refer to themselves as "Bushies," in the English version, with the "sh." For a while one was supposed to drop "Bushman" altogether, even when referring to the true-blue brand, in favour of "Khoi" or "Khoi-san." That seems to have faded, and lately there has been the beginnings of a "First South Africans" movement, which is of course mainly led by the kind of coloured people who look like Europeans with suntans.*

58. Tannie — "auntie," not implying any actual relationship. All younger Afrikaans people call all older ladies "tannie," causing great distress when they carry it over to urban English thirtysomethings who would rather be taken ☞

a TANT ANNA Ware[59] Skotse Whisky.

"That's the only Afrikaans Scotch you'll ever see," she says. "It's just a pity Carnarvon isn't a better place to keep whisky. It evaporates, you know, through the bottle."

My scepticism must show. "Don't look at me like I'm telling you tales," says Tannie Di, sharply. "Look here." She grabs a bottle and makes me scrutinise the seal. Virgin. "Now look at the level," she says. "A third down."

Well, in Carnarvon you can bake bricks without an oven. Anything's possible.

In the bar, discussion is about the activities of someone called "he." "He" doesn't need to be named, I learn. Carnarvon people can walk up to each other and say: "Have you heard what he's doing now?" and they know who you mean. You mean Ahmed.

Ahmed started off, by barroom consensus, as an Indian, with a little shop halfway between town and township. Somewhere in South Africa's maze of changing racial legalities he got himself reclassified as coloured,[60] so he could buy up the township. One school of barroom thought holds that this was a dirty trick, alarm bells should have started ringing. The alternative school, represented by one Fanus, a man with a wrist the girth of an average thigh, says this was fine, he was being smart.

Ahmed's township takeover did not cause much sweat on the white side of the tracks. But next thing anybody knew, he owned a shop in town, too, and then a garage, and then this and then that and now... well, this is big stuff. Now, the town's very epicentre is up for sale, the central business block, all 664 square metres of it, housing the Mutual, Louise's Florist, the

----

(58 CONTINUED) *for a niece than an aunt.*

59. *Ware, pronounced vaar-ra = genuine.*

60. *Coloureds and Indians, the smaller "middle" groups in the racial quartet, intersect at the fuzziest of the various ethnic borders and gave grey hairs to aparheid's egg-sorters. Plenty of people could fit equally well into either* ☛

Little Petunia Hair Salon, and the symbolic premises of Nasionale Wolkwekers, the wool-breeders' agency, monarch of the Karoo.

Who will buy? Who will bid? Who but Ahmed? Is the town to be owned by this man, who can't hire its hall or vote for its mayor?

Fanus, with whom nobody seems keen to over-argue, takes the long view: "Ag, be honest now. He's pulled finger while we've sat on our arses. If he left, we'd be a ghost town in six months. Anyway, what dirt did he ever do us?" His audience is unconvinced. One man says sulkily: "He did us no dirt because we never let him. Wait till he's the baas and we're the slaves. Then you'll see."

There is speculation on whether and since when Ahmed is allowed to buy white land. Nobody knows. "It's a bit late to worry about that now," says the sulky guy. "He owns half of it already, and in any case what does the law mean these days?"

When the party breaks up, I walk down the main road to the office of

----

(60 CONTINUED) *classification. Plenty more looked like one thing but were classified as the other. They, like everybody else, were in apartheid's heyday supposed to occupy property only in their "own" areas. This was hilarious, insofar as to corral Indian shopkeepers into approved corners of bureaucratic maps was overall as effective as ordering water upstream. It was also disgusting, in that the State would every now and then wind up its big fist and thump. Indians, homes and shops and all, would get shoved into ethnic ghettoes with names like "Orientia," ten miles out of town. It was also, of course, perverse. Frequently the white business community (the people who now say "I was always against apartheid, you know") vigorously supported the removal of the competition — the dislocation, the insult, the eviction from (and firesale disposal of) century-old homes — only to discover that six months later Orientia was booming and town was getting wrapped in cobwebs. In the Karoo there were and are extremely few Indians, all traders and nearly all rich, and very many coloureds, sometimes traders but not often rich.*

the town's lawyer, who is also the estate auctioneer and building society agent. He is not around. His office is staffed by two women under a gigantic portrait of Paul Kruger.[61]

Outside, a quick-eyed coloured youth is sitting on the pavement doodling patterns in the dust, wearing a red T-shirt inscribed "ROAR YOUNG LIONS ROAR"[62] I ask if he doesn't get a hard time going around town like that. He shrugs and says: "I think they think it's a soccer club."

Ahmed's not around either, in the musty shop that is still his headquarters, and time is beginning to press.

I get in the car and mull over the map. One of the men from the bar comes up and recommends the tar road, through Britstown. I say, thanks, but I'll go the Prieska way, I've never been there. He looks my car over. It is a distinctive vehicle, donged on every surface including the top, where I lost an argument with a low bridge. Properly viewed, these blemishes are beneficial — they free you from worrying about scratches — but they don't impress the uninformed, like this guy.

He says: "Just don't let this heap conk in before Prieska. You could grow old on the walk, heh-heh."

Heh-heh. Little does he know. This car has paid its dues. Beneath the skin it's spanking new.

The 100 miles to Prieska have nothing on the way but kudu warning signs. Personally, I haven't seen a kudu outside a game park since I drove railway 20-tonners in northern Namibia, when we barely noticed them

---

61. 19th Century Boer leader who sunk his teeth into the calf of the mighty British army where they stayed painfully embedded for two years more than anyone had believed possible. The Karoo at the time was theoretically on the British side.
62. In politically conscious society there was believed to be an underground revolutionary group called the Young Lions. I suspect the belief was more wish than fact, which may relate to why the law-abiding burghers of Carnarvon didn't get upset.

because we were spoiled by the experience of nudging elephants off the road, and I have sometimes suspected the kudu signs are a plot by the tourist board.

"BEWARE OF TORTOISES," though — *that* could be useful. The first Karoo tortoise I meet I think is a big round rock in the road. I steer away, am surprised to have misjudged, and steer again. When I realise the rock is mobile, I swing back like mad and there's a hollow moment before I recover the road. This could have been hard to explain.

"I hear you rolled your car?"

"You see, there was this tortoise ..."

Karoo meerkats are suicide prone, and so is a beautiful young springbok that stands in the road and watches me approach. Five yards from the springbok I'm crawling, and it's stiff as a statue, head cocked in a deceptive impression of alert wild wisdom. Then it takes a spectacular airborne leap and smashes into the barbed wire fence at the roadside. It's knocked flat, and lies on its back, whimpering. I am almost at it when it regains its feet and wobbles leerily into the distance.

In a hundred miles I encounter one car, a BMW rehearsing for the world land speed record. I see its dust cloud coming for fifteen minutes 0before it whooshes past. Also one donkey cart, drawn by one donkey and carrying several people, several beds, several chairs and a cupboard. It's stationary at the time, which is not surprising, and a dispute is going on, although whether between people and people or people and donkey I do not discover.

These, I assume, are swerwers — coloured-cum-bushmen people who've lived this land for centuries and now spend their days trudging in search of a baas who'll let them squat until he needs them no longer, or thinks better of it, or takes offence, and they pack up their carts and trudge again. One hears a lot about the swerwers, ranging from that they're now all settled with ID books and pension numbers to that they're more and poorer than ever. One day somebody's got to update the tale.

Prieska calls itself "The Jewel of the North West Cape." Maybe that was valid once, but builders have got at it. Prieska is rich enough to be ugly. The impoverished dorps, like Loxton, wither and die and make good-looking corpses. The better off, like Prieska, build. They flatten the one-storey hotels with stoeps and eaves, and erect aggressive fortresses in their place. They knock down the picturesque town hall to impress the district with a new one twice as large and half as pretty. They demolish the distinctive elegant shops and rush to join the Wimpyburger culture.

I take a circuit round the town and discover the nation's first cattle-gate, designed and developed in Prieska in 1926 and now mounted in the library garden. There's that, and there are thousands of coloured people sitting on walls and pavements looking bored, and that's about it. Not a lot makes me want to stay, but there are many signs to "Tourist Information," and I feel in fairness I should check.

Tourist Information is in the town hall and is flabbergasted to be asked for its wares. There's a great hunting and finally a slim blue brochure is rustled up. I learn that if I come back in six months, the Ria Huysamen Aloe Garden will be in bloom. Also that Prieska means "place of the lost she-goat" in Coranna.

"Coranna?" I ask the lady. She studies the word in the booklet. "I suppose that's Boesmantaal," she says.

I feel I've seen Prieska, but Prieska has other ideas.

The car won't start. I turn the key, and there's silence, not even a grind or gurgle.

There are moments when massive unemployment shows a silver lining. In no time, half of Prieska is pushing a battered combi at a fast trot along the main road. Even then it jerk-starts with odd reluctance, and when I pause to fish for tangible thanks it cuts out again. More pushing, and a cautious experiment shows that if the revs drop below 2,000 I'm at risk of stalling. The petrol jockey at the nearest garage finds himself uncomfortably replenishing the battery — stone dry, inexplicably — while the engine keeps roaring.

I point straight for Kimberley, along the tar, very responsibly.

After about a hundred kilometres there's a side road to the confluence of the Orange and the Vaal rivers. This, I can't miss. It's worth it; the merger of the two great arteries, gleaming wild and African in the cloudless sinking sun. It cries out to be swum in, but I chicken out. The car is up where the road ends, revving under the weight of a rock resting on the pedal. I envisage the explanations:

"I hear your car was stolen?"

"Well, you see, it was out of sight with the engine running while I swam in the river ..."

I get back to the main road and start making up time. Night is falling, I'm 600 kilometres from home, and I have appointments in the morning. I'm barely under way when a uniformed figure rushes out of the bush with hand upheld. Speed trap.

The policeman is trim and no-nonsense, coloured. In both official languages he asks for my language of preference. He props his elbow on the door, ready to write. My foot stays on half-pedal.

"Excuse me," he says, "would you mind switching off?"

"Um, it's like this," I begin, and out comes the story.

He puts down his clipboard and says I've had enough problems for one journey. The dutiful citizen in me knows he should pull me off the road, the fallible human says: Thanks.

"Drive safely," he says, "and watch out for kudu. They jump for the headlights. We just had a case, about 30Ks on. Meat everywhere; you couldn't tell what was person and what was kudu."

Vowing never again to call kudu warnings into question, I proceed on the remaining hundred kilometres to Kimberley. Half way there, the generator warning starts to glow, ominous but dim. Then the headlights start to fade, ominous but slow.

The warning grows brighter and the headlights duller and I'm needing to keep revs at 3,500, then 4,000, to see where I'm going. But I don't want to end up confused with kudu flesh, so I drop gears, and then again, and when

Kimberley's giant rabbit-hutch of a radio tower at last hovers up, I'm shattering the tranquillity of the region at full revs in second gear.

Day 26

KIMBERLEY'S CLAIM TO FAME IS A HOLE — THE WORLD'S BIGGEST man-made hole, I believe. Diamond-hunters dug it a hundred years ago, or at any rate their indigenous employees did, standing on shoulders and heads and corpses in the way that we hear is still or again happening in Angola now, and funding the rebel side of that tragic country's eternal war.

It's close to midnight. The hole is locked up and so are the garages. I find an open hotel and check in. There is an incredible racket coming from the TV room. I peer in and discover a crowd of tough Boers wildly cheering a black South African boxer fighting an American. A teenager rises with old-world courtesy to give me space on the arm of a sofa. I'm as touched by the gesture as by the Boers' non-racial home-town partisanship, but our man will have to make do without my support. Bed is calling.

In the morning the car starts, first kick, and limps thirty yards into the workshop of the nearest garage, where it elicits much hilarity. "*This!* This is not a *problem!*" says the man, full of the superiority of expertise, "this is an *adjustment.* Ten minutes' work."

I twiddle thumbs while the ten minutes is met, exceeded, and eclipsed, and the adjustment calls for ever greater supplies of tools and consultation and expletives. My presence becomes ever more sore thumb, especially since the car is right next to a sign which I suppose the proprietor's uncle acquired in a novelty shop in Disneyland circa 1930: "Rates — $1 an hour. If you watch — $2. If you help — $5."

Eventually I say I'll take a short walk. "Okay," mumbles a relieved voice from inside the engine compartment.

The museum is close by. It has a two-headed lamb and a five-toed pig, pickled in a jam jar. It also has numerous aged attendants and/or hangers-around who are delighted to find a fresh face to retell the few words Sir Ernest Oppenheimer[63] once said to them, or who have shaken Harry's hand and been re-living the moment ever since.

Their loyalty to De Beers is as feudal as anything this side of the Meiji Restoration, but it's tinged now with perplexity and betrayal. De Beers is leaving, pulling out quietly, glacially, bit by bit. Kimberley is still technically the company's Head Office, but in practice this is fiction. Power resides from butt to nozzle in Johannesburg, whence directors evidently make an annual pilgrimage for a formal "Head Office" meeting to humour the locals. Which

----

63. Ernest, humble Jewish boy aus Deutschland aus, knitted up first the diamond industry and then gold. Harry, his extremely soft-spoken son, consolidated the twin empires, De Beers diamonds and Anglo-American gold, brought everything from banks to motor cars into the fold, and was allegedly the world's richest man until the record-talliers discovered the Sultan of Brunei at about the same time as some cheeky Americans like Messrs Walton and Gates snuck up from the blind side. With some exceptions, Oppenheimer money has created new businesses out of nothing rather than changing the ownership of businesses that are humming along anyway. Had Ernest never come to Kimberley, many man-million years of jobs and creation would have been lost to South Africa. By 1989, Harry (who is barely 5½ ft tall) was the colossus of Africa and uncrowned king. Much bigger status than mere presidents or prime ministers.

might explain why the locals now indulge in a speculation that once was treason: Might it have been better, after all, if the early diamond free-for-all had ended up in competition and counter balance rather than in the stranglehold of the De Beers dynasty, probably the closest thing in human history to a total monopoly?

Argument rages, with deep emotion and by no means one way. Perhaps without De Beers a diamond would by now be just another coloured stone for which kids scrabble in patches, five rands per bucket. Perhaps Kimberley would be not a has-been city but a never-was city, without even its memories.

I extract myself to check on the adjustment's progress. The car is out being tested. It returns in a cowboy skid a few minutes later and true enough, it's going like a Boeing. The repair costs even less than the hotel bill, and before lunch-time I'm on my way. I pass the signs to the hole and resist the urge to agog anew at that great crater, which I had last seen years before, and at the awfulness that its digging must have entailed.

But fate has not yet finished its fun. I'm paused at the last traffic light before the Dutoitspan road, the homeward route out of Kimberley, when I recognise the name on the cross-street. This is where my grandparents-in-law had lived for decades in the century's youth. We have a picture of the house in the family gallery on our staircase. The least I can do is take five minutes to see if the house still stands. I park at the roadside.

A cursory stroll reveals plenty of ancient elegant timber homesteads, the kind that in Kimberley rank a distant second to their plate-glass and klinker-brick neighbours but would in Johannesburg cause much salivating, and long feature articles in *House & Garden*. Most of the properties are the offices of consultancies and agencies, titivated and smartened up to an extent that would look unnatural in a residence.

No single house clangs or even tickles the bells of recognition. I give up without a struggle, offering a moment of silent obeisance to my children's grandfather. Ian Snedden died long before I entered his daughter's life, and here in an uncertain distant street is the one and only time I have ever felt his presence in mine.

The starter grinds in merry confidence. The engine flares, stumbles, and falls into a sulk. We're having some sort of repeat of Prieska, and I'm beginning to feel like a latter-day Job, or the victim of a hoax. I look around in involuntary expectation that the Karoo's mechanics are clustered behind hedges, giggling hysterically.

Instead, a business meeting is emerging from the house alongside. Four or five up-and-about young men in smart suits disperse to their cars, laughing and bidding hearty farewells.

Too embarrassed to grind and hack at an unwilling engine in their presence, I pretend to be waiting for a passenger from the other side of the road. My act is evidently less than masterly. One guy, with his car door already open, calls out: "Do you need a shove?"

"Oh um," I reply, "er thank you," or words to that effect.

So here are the assembled scions of Kimberley's gentry working up a sweat behind a brown tin can which refuses to behave in a respectable manner. After a short push it starts, and cuts out. A second push and it cuts out again.

The businessmen perceive a challenge to their manhood. They leave their jackets in a pile on the pavement and push the car up a long incline. When it runs down the hill on the other side it starts and stays started. They wave at my mirror from the horizon. They are in surprisingly good spirits for guys now having to break into their day to take showers and change shirts.

Indeed they are in better spirits than their rescuee, who reckons this is now enough.

The car is purring; as normal as can be if not more so.

Science and sense are whispering practicalities, but they get no hearing. My innards are telling me that to see home before the turn of the millenium I must drive and drive now, and can think later about scrapheaps or trade-ins. No more stops no matter what.

Which is firm policy and lasts for about thirty seconds.

I must take two corners to get back to the Dutoitspan road. The first road is clear, easy, empty. Obviously no awkward hidden traffic jam can be cunningly mustered on the second.

Obviously. But what there can be is a strike. Thirty or so people are toyi-toying[64] and brandishing ill-spelt semi-legible cardboard placards about greedy bosses and living wages. They're all over the road.

I can keep up revs and push past, which has to come across as an angry union-bashing Statement and leave them thinking, "how can these whites hate us so much?"

Or I can risk another cut-out, which is what I get. The strikers turn out to be mainly women, who converge entirely unasked upon the car, missing not a beat in the singing and dancing program, and push. A rugby scrum they are definitely not, and when the first start turns into a false start, two large Boer policemen who are leaning casually against their motorbikes, watching the strike, join in, eliciting huge circus cackles from thirty female strikers and beads of perspiratory relief from one male motorist.

Back at the robot where my five minute detour began an hour ago, the engine draws breath. I leave town with blinkers against every distraction on

---

64. *The toyi-toyi is a weird shuffling dance-cum-march which made an utterly mysterious appearance in about 1985 and promptly became a symbol of black defiance. (It still is, to the frequent annoyance of the now black government.). Nobody has ever claimed to know where it came from or why it is called what it is called. It provokes strong and confusing emotions, sometimes even in the same person, such as myself. I can sometimes behold a toyi-toyi and feel my spirits sink; this pathetic lame little hop-skip is to be the substitute for reason, argument, debate, thought, enquiry? Other times, and often in virtually identical contexts, I can swell with warmth and fellow-feeling for the toyi-toyiers: They have so little in their lives; and can still find solidarity and affection. Mixed up, of course. But, then, this is Africa.*

land or air, with a goodly heap of memory; and with a strong sense of how dauntingly endless, albeit absorbing, a road lies ahead in the quest to make a success of this unlikely concatenation.

It is said you choose your friends but not your family. You love your family regardless. But that's only half the point. You don't choose your nation either. This is my nation. Bullies and gomtorrels and revolutionaries and racists, smiling labourers and selfless samaritans and trusting traders, uprooted swerwers and honest dealers and feudal serfs and dedicated healers, drunks and dimwits and ignoramuses and lost and lonely battlers for survival. This is my family.

IT WAS RUSH-HOUR IN JOHANNESBURG, AND ALL WAS WELL until the exit from the M1. Then the car backfired violently and the engine cut out. It restarted by the skin of its teeth, when I was almost at a standstill and cars behind were hooting angrily. It was a nightmare along Empire Road and then I had only one corner to turn for our regular neighbourhood garage.

Graaaaaaaaaak.

A light walk home.

Postscript

THE COMBI WAS FIXED ONE LAST TIME, AND RAN WITHOUT hitch or hiccup for two years. Then it disappeared from outside my wife's office on our main university campus. That night we went out to celebrate. We celebrated that nobody had been in the car. They'd stolen it cold, while it was parked. No guns through windows; no death or injury; hardly any trauma. Not to say that one escapes the chilled intestines in that split second between the quizzical "I'm sure it was in this row" and the livid "Bastards! Bring back the noose!" But it's small trauma and fleeting, even when insurance is absent and the consequence is a radical downscaling.

That's one of the weird plusses of a society where life is on the edge. An event which in somewhere like Canada would leave the victim feeling ravaged and assaulted causes, in South Africa, a night on the town.

For years we looked closely at every brown Starwagon on the road, until we got to know most of them by name or at any rate by their registration initials.

"Look! Look!" one child would yell, "There! I'm sure!"

"Naw," a sibling would yawn, barely glancing up, "That's RGR. You know, with the funny aerial and the pony-tail driver."

Bit by bit the initial adrenalin-flows slowed, eventually to zero. Finally the combi — Naledi, we had called it, meaning "star" in Zulu — was gone. It was kaput, history, palaeocrystic, an ex-combi, not quite buried but certainly gone. Mourning period over.

Which, of course, is when I found it. Blindingly unmistakable, displaying numerous distinguishing features from the Arabic sticker bequeathed by the Moslem owner before us (and for which every Moslem we knew gave us fiercely contradictory translations) to the wobble where a bad golfer restyled the right headlight's eyebrow. No two ways, this was my car.

Then again, what exactly was I to do with this information? The scene was a taxi rank. In fact, not so much *a* taxi rank as the mother of all taxi ranks, the one in Soweto outside Baragwanath hospital. This is the home ground of several extremely volatile taxi associations, the spiritual heirs of the Wild West's cowboy gangs.

Taxi wars start and end with startling suddenness, sometimes to do with logical squabbles over routes or pick-up points, sometimes for reasons — which may or may not involve bewitchings and spells — which no Commission of Enquiry will ever get to the beginning of, let alone the bottom. It's quite possible for rival taximen to start a day as friends, take a breakfast break for a quick shooting war which leaves several corpses, including some passengers who never knew that their sin was to patronise the wrong association, and spend the evening drinking beer together in the shebeen.

A taxi rank at peace is an oddly uplifting environment, full of bonhomie and brotherhood towards all mankind and not least the rare white face (which, unless in uniform, usually betrays a journalist or similar eccentric.) But it's not a good place to stand on high horses, or to quote literature, especially such literature as the citizen's arrest section of the Criminal Procedure Act No 56 of 1955 (as amended).

This thought was not far from mind as I contemplated the bashed and beaten face of a once cherished family artefact, repository of a myriad memories ranging from moonlight conjugals on mountain weekends to the time in the Kruger Park that we'd disturbed a herd of elephants and been splattered with spittle from an angry grey trunk fleetingly entrapped just outside a closing electric sunroof.

It was the middle of the day, down-time for the taxi drivers who enveloped us in their hundreds playing cards and dice until the afternoon rush hour. Many or most displayed ungainly lumps in the smalls of their backs. That's the fashion. Taxi cowboys don't wear six-guns in showy hip holsters like their forerunners. They carry them in their belts in the middle of their back. (Which to the outside eye seems an uncomfortable and impractical position. Let alone that in time of sudden need they have invisible coattails to negotiate, if the thing went off by accident you'd have a one-buttocked taxi driver.)

Was I to forage in search of a particular driver and say: "Excuse me but I'll have my car back now if that's okay?" Or to bustle off to the police station in the dim hope of returning with a posse, and the high likelihood that if that eventuality did transpire there would be a High Noon at the Bara Corral?

And if I wound up intact and hale and riding victoriously up the drive at Chez Beckett, what then? Once there would have been joy in the reunion. Now too late. A mere peep at the interior, tattered and awful, jolted me morbidly out of the nostalgic recollection of singalongs and snoozes. It would give the kids bad dreams. And the paperwork of recovery! The bureaucracy; the court appearances; the potential for dissuasive bullets to explore our street-facing windows.

What, too, if the current owner had bought the car in innocence, even the ask-no-questions brand of innocence that was the only "innocent" option on the menu? I was to remove his livelihood so that a distasteful pile of motorised scrap iron could clutter my driveway? Or so I could sell it to recover a fraction of what had long ago been written off?

All I knew for sure was: This car would to this family never again be what it once had been. I waved it fond farewell and left in peace.

With the Karoo, we're in much closer touch than before the Starwagon's mishaps. We feel at home now, at the stops on our pilgrimages to beaches and grandparents. And there are many more stops. We used to do the trip the macho way, start in the small hours and arrive for dinner. Now we take two days or three, with unhurried pauses at the Bed & Breakfast establishments that are proliferating everywhere. We've acquired a particular favourite, an ancient farmhouse with a duckpond and a raft on old barrels and a foefie slide — a cable on which you launch yourself from a high tree and scream like hell for thirty yards until you smack into the pond — but we explore others too, and constantly discover new and fresh and different.

Growth does take place, and it is well to keep that in mind because the other thing also takes place, and often seems to be streaking way ahead. Supposedly the new South Africa, with the dead hand of minority rule replaced by the glories of democracy and freedom and transparency and transformation, means rebirth and renewal. But then, that is also pretty much what Bolshevism was supposed to mean when it replaced the ills of Tsarist autocracy.

The theory and the reality do overlap here and there, but it's not a rule or anything. Employment shrinks, crime grows, and litter carpets the nation.

I did another round tour of the Karoo last year, by design this time, and as a journalist. I was horrified by much of it, and notably by Merriman station, which in the last days of the oppressive State was an attractive focal point, and has become in the first days of the democratic State a vandalised ruin. A local leader showed me around, and mumbled a long pathetic excuse to the effect that since the people have so little it is therefore to be expected that they will wreck what they've got. Sometimes a guy can wonder whether we have any way to go but down.

And then we pass through Vosburg, another little no-hope Karoo whistle-stop until we look twice, blink, pinch ourselves, and wonder why the place is looking as spring-cleaned as a movie set. The answer turns out to be extremely simple. It's because one single individual got up one morning, thought, "this town is looking disgusting," and set off on a one-man campaign to make it sing —cutting other people's grass and building other people's walls until bit by bit the whole town joined in.

I stand at the top of the hill looking over Vosburg in the sun's rich evening rays and think: "That's inspiration. That's why I love it here." Plus, of course, that we are extremely sure the one thing we will never die of is boredom.

Trekking: In search of The Real South Africa

The book behind the scenes of the author's popular television series, Beckett's Trek. Denis Beckett has never been known to shy away from the real issues of the day, no matter how controversial.

Madibaland

The second volume based on the TV series, this time a thoughtful and provocative account of the life and times of an intriguing nation. Beckett's voice is 'The work of an observer who tells it precisely as he sees it ...' — *Rapport*